JACOB'S LADDER

By

J. E. Muzzio

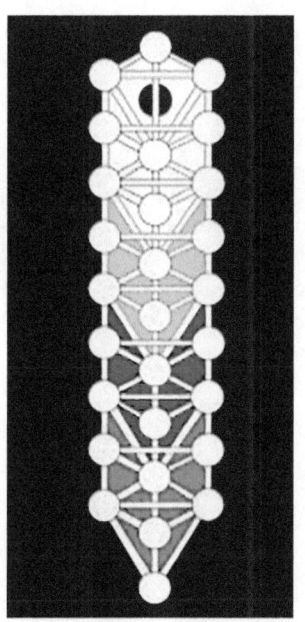

Jacob's ladder

Editors: Kimberly Rooks, Donna Melillo, Christian Pacheco.
Cover Design: 3-Sixty Design

Ordering Information:
Quantity sales: Special discounts are available on quantity purchases by corporations, associations, and others. For details, contact xxxxx

Library of Congress Control Number: 2017942278

ISBN: 978-0-9990210-0-2

Dedication

To Mrs. Richmond.

To my children, who often roll their eyes at me, I love you more than you will ever know.

To Mary Melinda, you are my sister, my friend, and my encourager. Thank you for always being my champion.

To Gloria, we have shared each other's sorrow, and we have found that we cast a shadow.

To Nancy, I miss you.

Acknowledgments

I would like to thank and acknowledge The One who created me from his imagination and my father and mother who made me from their love, I could not have created this story without that gift.

PROLOGUE

November 9, 2014

Tampa, Florida—The Cigar City where the sun rises over Davis Islands; three islands that were created of sand dredged from the bottom of the polluted Tampa Bay. The sand was then situated upon submerged foundations of garbage, discarded building materials, and more than one rotting corpse.

Davis Islands—the final resting place for victims of gangland slayings, a testimony to Tampa's claim to infamy. Nonetheless, it has some of the most beautiful sunrises in the country. As dawn burns through the morning fog, a young nun finds herself sitting on a cool, damp cement bench facing a spectacular sunrise. Life is escaping her body from a deep cut along the palm of her hand and across her wrist. Her blood is falling in large droplets and hiding in the folds of her heavy black clothing.

The woman's mind races as she surveys her surroundings. She turns toward the Tampa skyline. The morning sun reflects from mirrored twenty, thirty, and forty-story buildings.

"If I wrap my hand tightly, the bleeding will stop," she mumbles. She twists her hand into the dark fabric, and the bleeding slows. She lays her head on the back of the bench.

"I am alive…alive." *Her eyes close in a quiet surrender to pain and fitful dreams that take her to another place and time.*

Jacob set his jaw and looked only toward the monastery looming ahead. Dark clouds were building, a storm was brewing. He picked up his pace. They would have to hurry.

"Please, Father, *listen* to me! I can help. I want to go

with you. I am old enough, Father. I am sixteen years old, almost seventeen. I can help you. Please do not make me go there! I am strong and clever, Father. I am the cleverest girl in my class, and I am smarter than any boy." The words flying from Miriam's lips were falling on her father's seemingly deaf ears. "Please Father, let me go with you!"

Jacob drew a deep breath, glanced askew at his daughter, and strengthened his resolve. He took Miriam's hand to hasten their journey. Miriam pulled her hand from her father's grip, stepped back, and planted her feet firmly in the hardened sand of the dusty road.

"No! I will not go. I will not live there! I cannot be like them. I will not!" Miriam's resolve matched her father's.

Jacob turned to face his daughter. Now she could see the tears spilling down his cheeks. She could feel his heart breaking, as she searched his eyes they exchanged each other's sorrow.

Falling to his knees and taking his precious child in his arms, Jacob gathered every ounce of strength in his being to speak the words that he knew he must now speak. "Miriam

Ruth Davidson, give me your promise. Give me your oath this day before God. Swear to me that you will do what you must. Obey the sisters and learn their ways. Live as one of them. Swear to me, Miriam. Swear that you will seek to understand the existence that will be granted to you."

"I promise, Father." Miriam's tears fell as she gave her oath to her father in the presence of God. Now she is bound by her promise. "But tell me why I cannot go with you."

"You read my journal."

"I am sorry, Father."

"The days of sorrow shall renew themselves." Jacob cried as he held his precious child.

"The days of sorrow shall renew themselves," the woman whispers.

The southern sun climbs high into the Florida sky, growing fiercer with each leg of its journey. The cool, misty morning changes into the relentless pounding taskmaster of the afternoon.

From dawn through midday, the woman sits like an alabaster statue of a saintly nun from long ago. The cool damp cement bench beneath her has turned to a steaming stone oven.

Police Officers Vicky Knight and Mike DeAugustino respond to a call to investigate the strange specter that appeared at dawn and, hours later, still sits bewildered and frightened.

Vicky and Mike have been partners for six years. After a markedly nasty divorce, Vicky gave up on love and moved to the Tampa Bay area. Vicky has sworn to uphold the law and that no man will ever hurt her again she has been true to her word. Vicky is a real Georgia Peach a Southern belle with a 9mm pistol. Mike is a Tampa native, as were his parents before him and their parents before them. He grew up in Ybor City, the historic Latin district of Tampa. Mike's father was a Tampa vice detective. Mike will soon take the detectives exam, he plans to continue his father's investigation into the Vicente crime syndicate.

The police officers start across the Boulevard to the Bayshore promenade. Mike assesses the woman as they approach. Her face is framed in white linen.

Her head is covered by a black wool veil that falls past her shoulders and all but vanishes into the black of her heavy garb. She appears to be a vestige of a bygone conviction; her hazel eyes are still and lifeless. Her lips are dry and parched, and her fair skin is flushed, burned, and bruised.

"Whew," Mike whistles through his teeth. "Would you look at all of the regalia she has on? And you know she could have a weapon hidden under all that." Mike is cautious as he sizes up the woman.

"What sort of a weapon does a nun usually carry, Michael?"

"Depends on what order they're from." Mike grins. He loves it that Vicky calls him Michael. "Did I ever tell you about the time my friend Rolando and I dropped a firecracker down the toilet at the Sacred Heart School? Boy, did we suffer for that, but not as much as when we rolled the fire extinguishers down the staircase. We taped 'em open first." Mike chuckles.

As they walk, Vicky whispers. "Have you ever seen a nun who looks like that? She looks ancient."

11

Having been raised in the Freewill Baptist persuasion in southern Georgia, Vicky has little knowledge of nuns or anything else Catholic. For that matter, free will has been a fleeting fantasy to Vicky. It seems to her that the words "free will" and "Baptist" when strung together create the colossus of oxymoron.

"No, I've never seen one like that, not even when I was a kid at the Sacred Heart School. I've seen nuns like that in old pictures, sure, but not for real."

"You think she's real or what?"

"Or what."

"You're a smart ass, Michael. So, since you're so smart, you go on and take this one."

"What? No, she's a female. You should take it."

"She's a nun. You know more about nuns than I do. I'll take the next one."

"Okay, I'll hold you to that." Mike smiled he approaches the woman and begins questioning her. "Can we help you? Can you hear me, ma'am?" Mike's concern grows with each unanswered question.

"It looks like she's been out here for a while, Michael. Maybe she's from the monastery over in Kumquat."

"The Holy Trinity? She might be," Mike says, keeping his attention on the woman.

The Holy Trinity Monastery was built by Klaus Duetzman. He then donated it to the Catholic Church in a desperate attempt to atone for his wretched life and in the direst hope he would not spend eternity in purgatory—or worse. Klaus Duetzman has long since passed to his direst hope and probably worse, leaving his son Richard as patriarch of the Duetzman family. Richard, Red to his friends is now living his own wretched life amidst Tampa's high society.

It has been said of the Duetzman's that they have more money than God, not because they have so much money but because they have so little God. The Catholic Church teaches that the love of money is the root of all evil, yet the Duetzman family tree suckles unrepressed from that evil root and bears the fruit of that consequence.

To the gathering crowd of curious onlookers, Mike appears to genuflect in solemn respect to a holy icon as he drops to one knee and continues to question the young woman. "Can you tell me your name? Do you know where you are?"

From somewhere far away, she can hear the sound of a voice, a man's voice, bringing her back to this strange place.

"Do you know where you are?" the voice is asking. The woman wills her eyes to focus on the man kneeling before her. Fear and panic grip her as she realizes she is being questioned by a police officer. Her only hope to survive is to run, to hide.

The young woman struggles to her feet. She knows she must escape. She must find her father and the others then she will be safe. But she finds no escape, only darkness, as she collapses into Mike's arms.

"Roll EMS!" Mike shouts.

There are two sounds foremost in the woman's ears: the distant sound of a siren and the call of a raven.

As the EMTs lift the stretcher with the woman into the waiting ambulance, she turns toward the sound of the raven's call.

"Sandalphon…" she whispers as she returns to velvet darkness and dreams of sorrow.

"I love you, Miriam." Jacob held his daughter for the last time. Taking a small black leather book from his coat, he placed it in her hands. A blank journal bound with ties so pages could be added. The book was inscribed:

Hidden things belong to the lord our God but revealed things belong to us and to our children, forever.

Deuteronomy.

CHAPTER ONE

THE DREAM

Miriam stood with Mother Mary Gertrude in the garden behind the stone wall that secluded the sisters from the outside world. Through the heavy wrought-iron gate, Miriam watched as her father's tall, strong figure turned into a small dot on the horizon. With all of her being, Miriam wanted to run after him. She wanted to make him relent and free her from her promise to stay with the sisters. However, bound by the oath she had sworn to him, Miriam could only watch as he moved farther and farther from her. As he slowly disappeared, the crushing reality of her abandonment forced her to her knees. Clutching to her heart the journal her father had given her, she cried inconsolably.

"Father, Father!" Miriam quietly sobbed.

"Shh, do not cry, my darling." Mother Mary Gertrude knelt beside the crying child. She held Miriam, gently rocking the young girl as she tried to comfort her.

"What is to become of me?" Miriam looked into the kind and gentle eyes of the mother superior.

"Take heart, my child. God is watching. We will be strong together, ja?"

"Ja." Miriam cried.

Mother Mary Gertrude remembered the words she had spoken to her friend, Jacob: "With my life, I will guard your child."

Jacob Davidson walked toward his home. Only a short while ago he had walked this dusty road with his daughter. Miriam is Jacob's dearly loved only child. "Strong and clever." Jacob smiled as he remembered her words. Miriam *was* strong and clever. She was truly her mother's daughter. Sara Rosa, Miriam's mother, was the only woman Jacob would ever love. He was certain they had been created in the heavens as one person, split apart to be born into this life, and then drawn back together as man and wife to be one again.

Miriam was the miraculous result of that reunion.

As Jacob walked, he watched the dark clouds that had formed on the horizon. He felt the electricity in the air as the thunder rolled from cloud to cloud. Miriam had been ushered into this world on a night much like this. That night, the lightning split the sky. The flashes of light that followed, one after another, transformed the minute of her birth into a surreal string of moments in time. Then there she was— Jacobs hope, Miriam; glorious, screaming feminine principal.

Jacob followed the dusty road along the bank of the Danube. Just ahead, he could see his home, a small stone cottage on the grassy slope of the dark river. Only yesterday he had sat on that slope laughing and talking with Miriam as she picked at the clay that seemed to grow out of the riverbank.

"Heidi has not been in school for three days, Father." Miriam had said as her hands worked independently of any conscious thought, forming and reforming the piece of wet earth she held. *"I have gone by her house every day, but there is no one there. I think they have gone on holiday. We are*

best friends. I do not know why she did not tell me she was leaving. She tells me everything. One day in class, Heidi told me that their cow pushed over the rabbi's out building. And he was in it! We laughed until we cried. The teacher asked what we were laughing at, and I said that she told me a funny joke. So the teacher made Heidi come to the front of the class to tell it. Heidi told the whole class about the cow, the rabbi, and the out building, then everyone was laughing, except the teacher."

"Do you ever breathe, my child?" Jacob gently teased. Miriam looked down at the clay form in her hands for several moments before looking up at her father.

"Why were you talking to the mayor two evenings ago?" Miriam held her father's eyes with her own.

"This is very good, Miriam. You search my eyes for the truth. You will always find the truth in the eyes, for they are the windows of the soul." Jacob knew that he must now tell his daughter the truth for she had read his soul.

"Miriam, you know Wilhelm has been my friend since childhood, and his older sister, Emma, was like a second mother to me and to your Uncle Aaron. Wilhelm came to

warn me that there are people coming here to question us. He said that Aaron and I should leave town quickly."

"Where shall we go, Father?"

"I am sorry, Miriam, but you must stay. Aaron and I will go." Jacob turned away. He could not allow his daughter to read the fear in his eyes.

"What…what do you mean I must stay? I cannot go with you? What am I to do? I cannot wait here alone until you and Uncle Aaron return!"

"Wilhelm's sister, Emma, is the mother superior at the monastery. Wilhelm and I have made arrangements with her for you to stay there until it is safe."

"Father, I should come with you and Uncle Aaron. I can help you. I have been studying for almost a year now."

"No, Miriam, you cannot come."

"Father, please!" Miriam dropped the clay form from her hand into the wet sand of the riverbank, slumped to the grassy slope, and sobbed. Jacob knelt beside her and tried to make her understand why it was necessary for her to stay at the monastery. However as Jacob spoke Miriam sobbed all the more.

"My decision is final, Miriam. We leave for the monastery on the morrow." The discussion was ended. Jacob picked up the form that Miriam had dropped and studied it. She had transformed the piece of earth into the image of a large bird. "It is a raven."

"Yes. Does it look like Sandalphon?" Miriam sniffled.

"Yes, he does look like my childhood pet. He looks as if he could fly away at any moment."

"But you said Sandalphon never flew away from you even though he was not caged."

"No, he did not fly away. He trusted me, just as you must trust me now, Miriam."

"But, Father, why did Sandalphon trust you?"

"I think he knew he would have died on the ground if I had not chanced upon him when he fell from his nest."

Miriam moved closer to her father and laid her head against his arm. "Tell me again about Sandalphon, Father."

"Sandalphon was my only playmate before your Uncle Aaron was born. He followed me everywhere. He even played tag with me."

"How, Father? Tell me how he played."

"No matter where I happened to be, Sandalphon always found me. Upon finding me, he would fly down. I would try to catch him in the air as he swoop toward me, and then at the very last second he would avoid my grasp. He would play that game of tag for hours. He never seemed to tire of it."

"Now tell me about Sandalphon the spirit, Father."

" *"I am getting to that, child. Be patient." Jacob smiled. "Sandalphon is the spirit who stands on the first rung of Jacob's ladder. It is said that he is so tall that his head is in the heavens and is feet are on the ground," Jacob smiled down at his daughter and continued his story. "He is the guardian spirit of all humans. I will call this one Sandalphon also." Jacob studied his daughter's creation. Her mother's talent truly is in her hands.*

"Jacob, Jacob. Is it done?" Aaron met his brother at the edge of their small village.

"Yes, it is done." The sound of his brother's voice drew Jacob out of his memories.

Aaron looked to the dusky sky. "Come. We must

hurry. The sun is setting."

"We will meet here tomorrow morning before the sun rises, and then we will join the others," Jacob spoke quietly to his brother.

"Yes, brother. Is Auvil prepared to travel with us?"

"Yes, he is Aaron."

"Until the morrow then. Good Sabbath." Aaron hurried to his home before the sun set.

"Good Sabbath, Aaron."

Jacob entered his house and sat at his small table. He lit one candle, prayed to the God of the Universe, and held his glass to heaven in a toast to life. Then Jacob dropped his head and wept bitterly.

Before the appointed meeting hour, Jacob arose from his sleep, awakened by the approaching storm. The candle that Jacob had lit still burned. In the dim light he fumbled through his bureau drawer. He took a small box from the drawer; tears filled his eyes as he opened it. He then took a small silver vial and Sara Rosa's wedding ring from the box and held it in his large, strong hands. He placed the ring, a symbol of their love, on the bureau next to the clay raven. As lightning flashed and electricity filled the air Jacob read from his journal.

There was little chance that Jacob, Aaron, and Auvil would be seen as they pushed through the deep undergrowth of the Black Forest. It would take the men three days on foot to reach their destination of Freiberg, a port town on the Rhine River, almost seventy-five kilometers away. The men knew they must keep to the dense forest and not chance being seen in the open fields or on the highway.

As they walked, Jacob said, "I dreamed of Sara Rosa last night."

Aaron had heard these words from his brother many times before. He knew that every dream, every thought, and every remembrance of Jacob's beloved Sara was sacred.

"Yes, Jacob," Aaron looked into his brother's dark eyes.

"But this dream was much different than any dream I have ever had of her," Jacob said.

"Tell me how so, brother?"

"She spoke in this dream. She has never spoken to me in a dream before."

"Tell me the dream."

"I dreamed I went to my bed to sleep. As I slept in my dream, I had a dream. Do you understand that?"

"Yes, you had a dream within a dream. Tell me the rest Jacob."

"In this dream, I woke. I turned in my bed toward the wall. Upon turning I saw that the wall was no longer there. I could see a horse and wagon approaching my house. I arose from my bed. Then, at once I was standing outside."

"As I stood in the path, the horse and wagon came to a stop in front of me. You, Aaron, were the driver. I saw that Sara was sitting in the wagon. I walked to the back of the wagon so I could see more closely what she was doing. She was embroidering a scarf. As she made each stitch, I could see the pattern becoming ever more intricate. When she finished, the embroidered scarf had become a lace collar."

"I said, 'Sara that is so beautiful. What do you call that pattern?'"

"'Life,' she answered."

"Life? Why?" I questioned.

"This collar is highly sought after and brings a great price for its intricate design and delicate stitch. But often the design and intricacies become bothersome so the collar is wrapped in tissue paper and placed in a bureau drawer, awaiting a never appointed time to wear such an elaborate collar," she explained.

"Although I was afraid of her answer, I asked, 'Who have you made this collar for? Miriam,' she whispered as she offered the collar to me."

"I tell you, Aaron, my heart stood still as I put my hand out to receive the collar. When I took the collar, it ripped in half. I stood horrified. I saw the beautiful piece of torn lace fall from my hand to the ground. I watched as the half in Sara's hand fell between her fingers as it turned to dust. When I looked to the ground, the piece I had dropped was clean and new and had become a whole collar again. I looked up and Sara was gone. Then, I awoke. Can you tell me the meaning of this dream?"

Aaron watched Auvil lumbering through the thick underbrush. "Do you think he is able to talk?" Aaron asked as the Herculean figure of a man plowed through the thickets oblivious to the brambles and branches.

"Auvil? I don't know he never has. It seems he has no need to talk. But what about the dream?"

"Let me think about it."

Three days later, Jacob, Aaron, and Auvil met five others at the river dock. Hiding in the predawn shadows, they watched as Captain Peter Von Dague, a Dutch trader, and his first mate Morris Taylor load cargo onto the barge moored to the landing.

"No, not that one!" Captain Von Dague stopped his shipmate as he picked up a crate lying off to the side and began to load it into the barge. "That one's our ace in the hole." The captain whispered to his first mate with a smile and a nod. They exchanged knowing glances and continued loading the cargo boxes that lined the dock.

"Good morning," Lieutenant Heinz Reichmann of the dock patrol addressed Captain Von Dague in a genial manner.

"Good morning, if you can call it that. With all this cargo and the fog slowing us, it's been a hell of a morning, a hell of a morning indeed," Captain Von Dague grumbled good-naturedly. "I see you have your new right-hand man with you."

The young officer smiled, delighted to be recognized as an important addition to the dock patrol.

"What have you got here? This one has no dock stamp on it." Lieutenant Reichmann gestured to the ace-in-the-hole crate—the crate that Von Dague had put aside specifically for this purpose. "Open the crate," Reichmann ordered.

"Ja, let's have a look." Von Dague broke open the crate, revealing a case of Green Fairy, an opium-based absinth.

"Green Fairy, where did you get that? I have not seen any of this for almost twenty years!" Reichmann exclaimed.

"A Frenchman came across a whole cellar full of the stuff, I was lucky to acquire it from him. Ja, damn lucky," Von Dague said.

"Still, you have no dock stamps. Tell me, did you say the Frenchman has more of this?" Reichmann asked.

"A whole cellar full, I think I said. Certainly enough for everyone here," Von Dague repeated as Reichmann studied the case of rare liquor and weighed his options.

"Listen, my friend," Reichmann began. "If you give me three bottles of this, we will both go away happily and then perhaps you will remember me the next time you have a case of this."

"Three bottles, hmm? You drive a hard bargain, a hard bargain for certain, but well worth it for the price I will get for the rest." Captain Von Dague handed the three bottles to Reichmann and the young officer.

"Enjoy," Von Dague called out as the soldiers hurried to their post, anxious to sample their contraband.

"I have only heard of this liquor," the young officer confessed, upon reaching the post.

"Then this will really be a treat for you." Reichmann laughed, as he pried the cork out of the bottle with his pocketknife.

Two hours later, Reichmann and the young officer were unable to make even one more toast to the Fatherland as they slumped to the floor of their post in a drunken opium stupor. As the dawn broke Captain Peter Von Dague and his first mate, Morris Taylor, were under way with their hold full of cargo, contraband liquor, and eight men hiding in crates.

"THE KING IS A BLOODY FAGGOT."

Peter Von Dague did not know if this statement was true, nor did he care. But Morris Taylor, the brooding hulk of an Englishman whom he had been drinking with all night, took offence to the toast that was raised in the crowded Irish pub by the drunken American pilot. The bar brawl that ensued banded their friendship forever.

"That was a bloody good fight." The Englishman sputtered through loosened teeth and a bloodied lip.

"Sign on with me Morris. I could use a good first mate, one with more brawn than brains." Peter Von Dague laughed.

"Aye, aye, Campth." Morris saluted Von Dague, and smiled a crooked smile through his swollen lip.

"Where are we taking them?" Morris asked Von Dague as they stood on deck, watching the dark waters of the Rhine sacrificing itself to the bow of their ship.

"They are trying to get to England. They have come on foot from a town about 75 kilometers away. I've made arrangements for a Dutch vessel to pick them up in Rotterdam and take them to Port Carmarthen, England."

"I guess everyone is running somewhere." Morris kept his eyes on the water."

Von Dague took a long drag on his cigarette, flicked the butt into the water and watched as the current carried it away.

"I'm going below. It's safe to let them out of the crated now."

CHAPTER TWO

AUVIL

"MAN OVERBOARD! MAN OVERBOARD!"

Morris yelled. He ran to the alarm and sounded the shrill

whistle. Von Dague, Jacob, and the others raced to the ship's

rail where Morris stood.

"Morris, ready the dingy now!" Von Dague ordered.

"Aye, Captain." Morris raced to the dingy and

checked the cinch to the hoist.

Von Dague lowered the dingy into the water. Morris

rowed toward the floating man. He grabbed the floating man's

arms and pulled him into the small boat. Morris then rowed

back to the ship. The dingy was hoisted back up onto the ship.

Morris and Von Dague pulled the man from the dingy onto the

deck; Jacob for the first time saw the man's face.

"Aaron!" Jacob pushed through the men and dropped to his knees beside his brother. "Aaron, Aaron!"

Seth, the physician traveling with Jacob and the others attended to Aaron. Aaron spewed water, and then with several more hacking coughs, he spewed a bit more.

"That's a nasty bump he's got there. But I'd say he's lucky, damn lucky. Most don't bob back up after a fall into this muddy brine. Sure damn lucky, I'd say." Captain Von Dague turned to Jacob and walked him out of Aaron's earshot. "Keep him below, warm and dry. This could go bad real fast. I've seen it before. Ja, real bad, real fast."

"My head. . ." Aaron looked to his brother.

"Morris, help take him below."

"Aye, Captain."

"Aaron, what were you doing? What happened?" Jacob asked as he, and Morris guided Aaron into a dry corner of the cargo hold.

"My scarf. It blew overboard and got stuck on the ship. I thought I could reach it, but I fell over the rail and hit my head. I guess my scarf is lost."

"No, Aaron, I have it. Morris fished it off the side of

the ship with a pole." Jacob finished dressing his brother in the dry clothes and wrapped the scarf around him.

"A pole. That easy, hmm?" Aaron smiled sheepishly, closed his eyes, and gave himself over to exhaustion.

"Auvil, stay here and watch Aaron. I must speak to Seth again."

"Will he be all right?" Jacob asked Seth.

"I am afraid his skull is fractured, Jacob. There's nothing I can do. Keep him dry and warm. It is in God's hands now."

"Thank you, Seth."

"I will come back to check on him again later." Seth returned to the quiet conference of the other men. Jacob returned to Aaron.

Aaron opened his eyes and looked at his brother sitting next to him like a sentry. Jacob leaned forward and adjusted Aaron's scarf.

"When you gave this scarf to me, so you would have an excuse to buy another from that Gypsy woman, I was worried. I never told you, but I went to the market to find her. You did not know this. I went to tell her that she is not one of us and to resist your advances. I knew it would be of no avail to tell you. You would not have listened to my advice, Jacob. You have always thought with your heart."

"But Aaron, you loved Sara."

"I did. That day, when I went to the market, I was expecting to find a thief. Instead, I met a beautiful, young woman who looked into my eyes. She looked in my eyes…" Aaron's eyes closed.

Jacob spoke to Auvil, who sat stoically at Aaron's feet.

"When he was a baby, I watched him as he slept. He was so little, I thought I would for all time be his big brother. I vowed to always watch over him. I kept my vow. Even as he grew, I looked after him. However, at some point, that changed, and he became the one who was watching over me. I knew Aaron was concerned when I met Sara Rosa, but he remained silent about his concern. He accepted Sara Rosa for my sake at first, but he grew to love her. I, on the other hand, I fell in love with her the minute I looked into her eyes. She was truly my split-apart."

"The dream, I know what it means." Aaron looked

into Jacob's eyes and beyond.

"Quiet now. Tell me later."

"No, now. I must tell you now."

"Aaron, please."

"No. I must tell you now. I am not afraid of what is to come. Life, Jacob, the collar—it is about life. It is your life, Miriam's life, and Sara's life all woven together and then torn apart. Your life is out of your hands. Miriam's life has been made new, and Sara's life is gone...dust. Jacob, I tried to save her. We heard the glass breaking. We ran, but there were too many of them, too many... I tried to save her. I tried. Please forgive me, Jacob. Forgive me."

"I forgive you, Aaron. I forgive you," Jacob whispered as Aaron closed his eyes to sleep in the bosom of Abraham.

"*Seth*!" Jacob called across the crowded cargo hold. Seth hurried to Jacob's side. He searched Aarons neck for a pulse.

"I am sorry." Seth covered Aaron's body.

Jacob sat in front of Auvil, rocking forward and back as if he were petitioning at the Temple Mount Wall.

"Is there even one small crevice for my prayers,

Auvil? No, I think not." Lifting his eyes toward heaven, unable to contain his grief, he cried, "My God, I have mightily loved you. Since the day of my understanding, I have served you. I have followed your precepts, and I strive to keep your commandments. Now, I have lost my family, my home, and my country. Even so, my God I remain your faithful servant. Although it appears that I serve an unjust God, I will continue in my understanding, knowing that you will vindicate yourself and my faithfulness.

Seth sat next to Jacob and quietly listened while Jacob openly mourned Aaron's death. Jacob would be allowed a year of mourning according to tradition, but now they needed to talk. They needed to plan; they needed to talk to Von Dague. There would be time for mourning later.

"I am sorry, Jacob. Aaron was a good man and a true friend. This is a terrible loss. He will be missed." Seth was truly saddened.

"All he wanted was my forgiveness. He wanted my forgiveness for something he had no control over. The night Sara died, Aaron was with her."

Seth listened as Jacob's story brought back the horror

of the night of the broken glass.

"Every week, for years, Sara baked an extra loaf of bread for an old woman who lived less than a kilometer from our home. Usually, she finished baking early, but she had not seemed herself that day. It was getting late, but she promised she would hurry. She said she had something important to tell me when she got home. I suggested to her that she would be much quicker if Miriam stayed with me. I was anxious to hear what delicious foolishness she had contrived. Then, I made her promise she would hurry along and ask Aaron to walk with her."

"They made the journey to the woman's house. They left the bread with the woman, and just before the sunset, they began their walk home. Then, suddenly, motorcycles raced through the town. They came from every street and alley, the riders smashing every window and door as they rode through the town. Aaron and Sara heard the glass breaking. Everywhere they turned, there were fires from the oil lamps that had fallen, and broken glass that had been smashed from windows littered the streets. Some of the men saw Aaron and Sara run into an alley and followed them. They overtook

Aaron, beat him, and left him for dead. Sara, they found hiding only a short distance from where they had left Aaron."

"When it was quiet, I went to the streets searching for Sara and Aaron. I was hoping against hope that they had been at the old woman's house when the nightmare began. I found Aaron in the alley, unconscious and badly injured. Sara, I found dead. I fell to my knees in a sea of broken glass. As I held her lifeless body, I screamed these words of the psalmist to the heavens…VINDICATE ME, OH GOD, AND PLEAD MY CAUSE AGAINST AN UNGODLY NATION. WHY DO YOU CAST ME OFF? WHY DO I GO ON MOURNING BECAUSE OF THE OPPRESSION OF THE ENEMY?"

"Jacob, I am sorry, but we must talk with Von Dague now," Seth interrupted." Soon we will be in Rotterdam, and plans must be made."

"I understand. The lives of many are at stake." They all knew the importance of reaching England soon, very soon.

In the privacy of the captain's cramped quarters, Seth and Jacob sat with Captain Von Dague. The captain poured the men a glass full of Irish whiskey. Jacob spoke first, Von

Dague downed his drink before Jacob started his sentence.

"How long before we reach Rotterdam, Von Dague?" Jacob asked.

"Tomorrow, early afternoon. Ja, afternoon is the earliest I can get there. I have to keep to my regular schedule, so as not to arouse suspicion. Regular schedule, ja, puts us there tomorrow afternoon early." Von Dague poured himself another glass of whiskey. Seth and Jacob declined.

"Suit yourselves." He set the bottle down. "I have two sets of false mariner's papers. When we reach port, your men will leave the ship, two at a time, with the false papers. Morris will escort them to the waiting ship. Morris will then return with the false papers and continue accompanying your men until they are all safely aboard the ship, and then you will be on your way to merry old England."

"What about Aaron?" Jacob said.

"Don't worry. I'll take care of him as if he were one of my deck hands. I will say he died en route and has no family that I know of. Ja, none I know of. No one will question this. It happens often. Ja, often."

Jacob trusted Von Dague because he trusted his friend,

the mayor. Wilhelm Herder had not only warned Jacob and the rest of the men of trouble, but had also arranged for their escape. Auvil and Jacob would be the last two men to leave the ship. Seth and Ethan would leave first. The others would follow as Von Dague had said.

It was five o'clock, and Von Dague was getting nervous. Morris had left the ship more than an hour ago. He should have been back. Jacob and Auvil, the only two men left on board, should have already been on their way to the waiting ship. This trip had been a royal pain in the ass. First, the logistics of hiding the men in the restricted space of his cargo hold was a daunting task, and eight men were more than he had ever moved at one time. Then, the accident and a body to dispose of and now Rotterdam was crawling with seaport police. Ja, a royal pain in the ass. The police had been doubled since the last time Von Dague had been in port, and they were apparently searching for something. Something was wrong. Still, all in all, he would do the same thing over again. Von Dague would do it over again because he could not abide the maniacal ranting a madman. He would not salute nor would he pledge allegiance to this evil little man.

"Heil Hitler, my ass," Von Dague swore.

From the vantage point on the bridge of his ship, Von Dague watched the port police as they boarded and searched each vessel docked in the Rotterdam port. Now, it was his turn, and Peter Von Dague met the soldiers at the gangplank.

"We have orders to search this vessel. Stand aside," the arrogant young captain barked his orders to Von Dague. The four soldiers stood on the deck of Von Dague's ship.

"Help yourself." Von Dague knew that Jacob and Auvil would not be easily found. They had hidden themselves behind the ship's false wall, the wall that he and Morris had built for an occasion such as this.

"You two guard the deck while we search the cargo hold," the captain ordered. Von Dague led the officer and one soldier into the belly of the ship. The men stood in the hold surrounded by crates.

"What is all of this?" the officer said as he looked around.

"Moving crates. Some are empty. Some are full. That is what I do, move belongings. A lot of people are moving

42

these days. Ja, a lot of people moving. The neighborhood has gone all to hell if you ask me." He smirked at the men standing beside him. Von Dague knew that this was a dangerous game. He also knew that he must not show even the slightest hint of fear. The officer studied Von Dague for an extended moment.

"Who is this?" the officer asked, pointing to Aaron's body.

"That's a stupid bastard who's dead." Von Dague sat on an empty crate and lit a cigarette.

"What happened?"

"The stupid bastard fell overboard." Von Dague exhaled. A heavy cloud of smoke hung in the air over his head.

"Why is he still lying here? You have been in port for more than five hours according to our records."

"He got himself killed on my time, and he will get himself buried on my time. I am a busy man, and he is not going anywhere. I have no time to waste. Ja, he is not going anywhere." Von Dague extinguished the burning cigarette in the palm of his hand and dropped the butt into his shirt pocket, never breaking eye contact with the young officer. After the crates and boxes were thoroughly searched and inspected, the officer and the soldier turned to make their ascent back to the deck. Then, as if on some secret cue, they turned back to Von Dague.

"There is one more thing."

"What is that?"

"Take his pants down."

"What?" Von Dague was caught off guard by this request.

"The stupid bastard, take his pants down." The officer smiled as he mocked Von Dague.

"Sorry. Not interested. But help yourself."

"Do not play the fool, Captain. Take his pants down, and if he is not cut in the way of the Jews, then there is no problem. If he is cut, then there will be certain questions to be answered. I am sure you understand." The officer granted a vicious smile.

Behind the tallest stacks of cargo crates, there was just enough room to squeeze between the boxes. There was enough room to open the false wall and stand in the small space between the hull of the ship and the false wall. Jacob and Auvil stood in that space. Jacob watched through a small crack in the wall. The officer and the soldier stood with their backs to the hiding place. The officer stood very close to Von Dague. The other soldier stood more than a meter behind.

Von Dague bent over Aaron's body and reached for the waistband of Aaron's trousers. Von Dague struggled with the catch on Aaron's pants. The impatient officer leaned closer. When the officer had been manipulated in position, Von Dague brought his elbow up sharply into the officer's solar plexus. The officer lost his breath and rocked backward for a moment, enough time for Von Dague to pull the officer's pistol from its holster, but not enough time to shoot.

The officer tried to regain control of the weapon. The soldier standing behind drew his pistol but could find no opportunity for a clear shot at Von Dague. He followed the wrestling match like a deadly referee. Jacob watched with his hand on the release bar that opened the wall. Auvil watched Jacob.

The soldier stepped backward, tripping over a stack of boxes. At that moment, Jacob pushed open the wall and rushed toward the soldier.

Auvil advanced as the soldier turned and took aim at Jacob. In a matter of seconds, Auvil lifted the soldier over his head as if the man were weightless. The soldier's pistol fell to the floor just before his broken body fell from Auvil's hands.

Jacob recovered the soldier's pistol. The port hatch opened. The two soldiers who had stood guard on deck hurried down the ladder to investigate the noises coming from the cargo hold. Shots rang out, and the soldiers fell, victims of their comrade's pistol in Jacob's hand.

The officer and Von Dague continued their struggle for the weapon. Another shot rang out. Von Dague and the officer stood frozen in a deadly embrace. The officer smiled into Von Dague's eyes.

The smug look of victory turned to confusion and then disbelief. Blood trickled from the officer's mouth as he fell to join his troop in the ranks of death. Morris withdrew his dagger from deep within the officer's back.

"Sorry I'm late, Captain." Morris stepped over the dead officer.

"This is a bad one." Von Dague leaned against a cargo

box clutching his bloodied chest. The officer's bullet had found its mark.

"No, Captain. We have too much to do yet." Morris caught his captain as he fell.

"Make it so, Morris…" Von Dague gave his last command. Morris gently laid his captain's body next to Aaron. Then he stuck the dead officer's pistol into his pants.

"Jacob, the two lanterns in the corner and the box of flares, get them up top." Morris opened the tool locker and selected a very large pipe wrench.

Two pipes ran transverse overhead of the cargo hold. One pipe was the ship's fueling line, and the other, the gas line to the galley stove. While Jacob and Auvil stood on deck, Morris worked the fitting of the fuel line loose, spilling hundreds of gallons of fuel into the cargo hold. Then he opened the gas line and raced up the ladder. Considering what had just transpired below, it was amazingly quiet in port. If anyone had heard the gunshots, they did not know where they had come from. The men had little time to act, and Morris obviously had a plan. Morris bounded through the cargo hatch and closed it behind himself.

"Give me the flares." Morris tore open the box, shoved it next to the cargo hatch, and laid one flare over the side of the box. "Jacob, give one lantern to me and take the other to the gangplank." Morris opened the well of the lantern and poured a trail of kerosene from the box of flares next to the cargo hatch to the lantern at the gangplank. "Now we walk off the ship like we're going to tea!"

Morris lit the lantern at the gangplank and followed Jacob and Auvil. From the dock, Morris turned, drew the dead officer's pistol from his pants, and shot the burning lantern. The fire from the broken lantern followed the line of kerosene to the flares. The fireworks that ensued sent an invitation to every soldier in port to board the ship. As the fireworks displayed, soldiers swarmed the vessel. Curious to investigate the cargo hold, a soldier opened the hatch.

As thundering explosions, bellows of smoke, and walls of fire filled the sky behind them, Jacob, Auvil, and Morris walked toward the safety of the waiting ship.

"What the bloody hell are they so anxious to find?" Morris wondered aloud.

"They are interested in what we have done." Jacob

offered a vague answer. Morris was not satisfied.

"What is it that you have done that has enraged them so?" Morris demanded an explanation.

"It is not so much what we have done as how we have done it that interests them."

Morris stopped walking and faced Jacob. "You better come forth with an explanation pretty damn quick."

"It would be better if I show you. Auvil, come this way." Jacob directed his companions into an alley just ahead.

As they stood between the giant cargo boxes in the deserted alley, Jacob took the dead soldier's pistol from his coat. He turned the firearm in Morris's direction. Before Jacob could be stopped, he rang three shots into Auvil, who stood behind Morris.

"Have you gone mad?" Morris turned, braced to see Auvil lying in a heap on the alley floor. "What the bloody hell? He's standing . . . There's no blood. That is impossible! He has three bullets point blank in his middle!"

"We should hurry to the ship. I will explain later." Jacob started out of the alley. Morris grabbed Jacob by the arm and swung him around.

49

"I want bloody answers!"

Auvil stepped between the two men, breaking Morris's hold. "It's all right, Auvil." Jacob intervened before Auvil could act.

"I want an answer *now!*" Morris demanded.

"He is a golem. I made him. Can we go now?"

"No, we can't go now, and what the hell is a golem?"

"Morris, any minute, the police will come looking. I will explain once we are safely aboard the ship."

Morris sat on a crate in the alley, lit a cigarette, and inhaled deeply. He studied his burning cigarette. "I had thought of quitting. Nasty habit, but it's been a tough day. The ship is only a few hundred meters away. However, you can't board without me." Morris took another long drag on his cigarette. "Until I have an explanation that's to my liking, I'm not going anywhere. I think I'll quit tomorrow, maybe tomorrow."

Jacob decided he had better talk and talk fast.

"A golem is a soulless being created for protection. The others and I are Kabbalists, Jewish mystics. We have the knowledge to create these beings. We are traveling to

England to join with the Alchemists. We will work with them against the Fuehrer and the German war agenda. The psychic adviser to the Fuehrer has warned him that we will be a formidable deterrence to his ambition to cross the channel. They want to stop us from reaching England, and they want our knowledge in order to create an army of golems."

Morris set his gaze on Jacob and Auvil, the cigarette he drew heavily on burned almost to his fingertips. Morris crushed the cigarette beneath his foot.

"We better hurry."

CHAPTER THREE

IN THE COUNCIL OF MANY

"JACOB! Welcome, please sit at our table we have much to discuss."

Alden seated Jacob and the other men around a large oval table in the middle of a dimly lit room that was once a root cellar. It was not a large cellar, and it remained damp and dark, lit only by a few modest lanterns. The cellar tucked under a barn in the English countryside was hidden away from prying eyes and was now readied into a makeshift laboratory. The walls were crowded with shelves, each one teeming with the apothecaries' glass beakers and corked bottles. The array of bottles addressed every size, color, and form conceivable. The bottles, crucibles, and retort were readied on the shelves all the while screaming to the Alchemists, "Choose me; I am the secret to the elixir of which you search." However the Alchemists pay no heed to the willful cries. They just silently and persistently seek, as is their institution.

"I am relieved to finally see your face, Jacob. I heard there was trouble in Rotterdam."

"Yes, my friend, we lost Aaron and Von Dague."

"I am sorry. They will be missed. It is a great loss. And you, Jacob, how are you faring?"

"Thank you for your kind words Alden. Losing Aaron has been devastating, but I do not yet have time to mourn. Even though I suffer now, there are many in need of my help, as a result for the benefit of the living I must put off my sorrow. There will be much time in the future for my grief."

"What of Morris?" Alden asked.

"Morris traveled with us, and he vows to continue the work he and Von Dague started."

"And our friend Wilhelm? I trust that you left him well, fat, and sassy." Alden's cheeks pinched his eyes closed when he grinned.

"He remains well and continues to take advantage of

his aristocratic ancestry to keep himself safe from accusations of treason."

The conversation came to a lull as Alden hung his head, and Jacob breathed a deep and mournful sigh. The Alchemists and the Kabbalists were keenly aware that the world and even the heavens have been beset with horrors that were only to just begin.

"Jacob, do not worry. I am certain that Wilhelm and Morris will be arranging transportation for a time yet. Now, tell me Jacob, I must hear of the golem. How is he holding up? Has there been any deterioration? Does he continue to obey?" Alden was anxious to get to the heart of the alliance that the Alchemists and the Kabbalists had entered into.

"Auvil is holding up very well. Although it has been more than a year since we created him, I have not seen any deterioration. Furthermore, he never fails to follow my commands, and he seems to have a sense about my needs. I am curious if he will have a sense about you also since it was the combination of your elixir and my knowledge of golems that completed him."

"He is amazing, Jacob. No one would think he is

anything other than a mere man. Amazing." Alden shook his head in wonderment.

"Yes, he is amazing, Alden. I think he is perfect for the work we will be doing, he is very much a human being and equally as much a spiritual being. It is your living essence that we have added to our traditional creation of a golem that has allowed us to create this being."

"This is an exciting time for us in alchemy." Alden said. "For centuries, we have sought to form a truly human and equally spiritual being. Unfortunately all we could create are the Homunculi."

"Where are the Homunculi now?" Jacob was curious about the tiny creatures that the Alchemists had created.

"The Homunculi were weak and terribly difficult to sustain. They have all deteriorated, just as well I say. Those fellows are useless, disobedient and quite ill-tempered." Alden looked to his colleagues for confirmation. The Alchemists laughed as they agreed among themselves.

"We will begin our labors in the morning, Jacob. However, before we begin we will go to the village market. There I will introduce you to our trusted vendor. Then we will return to the cellar to set in motion our effort. I am anxious to start, but first we must all get a night's rest. Come, I will show you our quarters."

Jacob, Alden, and the unlikely troupe of Kabbalists and Alchemists filed out into the dark night of the English countryside. The Kabbalists were welcomed into a quite large and well-kept barn that sat above the cellar.

"These are our quarters, as you see they are spacious and afford enough room for all of us." He bent down and picked up a handful of clean dry straw. "And there is all the straw you can sleep on and more." Alden smiled as he allowed the straw to slowly fall from his fingers. In Jacob's mind's eye, he saw an image of Miriam as a young child playing with her puzzle sticks, trying and retrying to pick up the sticks, one stick at a time, without disturbing the next—a frustrating improbability.

"Thank you, Alden. I am very grateful, as are my men. We are also very tired from our journey." Jacob closed his eyes for a moment, not in exhaustion but to dismiss the vision of Miriam.

"Yes, yes, of course, Jacob. You and your men will

find a storage room full of horse blankets. Feel free to use what you need."

"Thank you, Alden."

"Don't thank me. Thank the aristocrat's horses. Their master, Lord Smithe, has put them out of their palace and allowed us in to stay in their stead." Alden laughed a hearty laugh.

Only a short time later, the barn fell silent, save for the sounds of men in fitful sleep. As the men slept, Jacob quietly spoke.

"Auvil, listen to me now and remember. Beginning on the morrow, you will have two masters, Alden and me. You must follow Alden's every command. Obey him and protect him just as you protect me. I must sleep now, Auvil." Jacob closed his eyes, and Auvil watched.

The rooster's song clamored in the men's ears. The cock's intention to welcome the dawn also served to warn any nefarious rival to be aware that he is the undisputed lord of the yard, and in due course his boast brought the sleeping men reluctantly to their feet.

"Good morning," Alden greeted Jacob. "There is bread and cheese in the cellar for our breakfast; afterwards we shall go to the market in the village.

The journey through the countryside to the small village was pleasant and afforded Jacob and Alden much time to discuss the daunting task that they would soon embark upon.

"I believe that Auvil will work well with you, Alden. I ordered him last night to obey you, although I believe he would have anyway."

"Good. Jacob, I am certain that we will all work well together."

"Yes Alden I believe so. We will be a commanding force against Hitler's agenda to cross the channel."

"Jacob my friend, merely the fact that Hitler is so determined to learn the secret of Auvil's creation and to destroy us and any other like us attest to the strength of our opposition to him. That is our village just ahead," Alden said. "The first vendor we will visit is a trusted friend, but beware there are whispers of Nazi sympathizers here, so we must be careful. I will introduce you as my cousin. It is best if only you and I come to the market. There is no sense in drawing undo attention to ourselves."

"I understand."

Alden smiled and headed into the market. Jacob followed Alden to the vendors table where Alden greeted a particularly hairy and generously wide man with a grin and a bear hug. Alden wrestled away and introduced Jacob. "Henry, old friend, this is my cousin Jacob, the one that I told you about." Alden spoke in an uncharacteristically loud voice for the benefit of any curious eavesdroppers.

"Jacob, good to meet you. Alden speaks of you often." Henry shook Jacob's hand, and in doing so, he pulled him close and whispered "Alden has told me that you and your men have arrived with only the clothes on your backs. May I send clean clothes to the barn for you and your men? Are you and the others of a similar stature?"

"Thank you, Henry. It is good to be here. I trust we will all become powerful friends." Jacob followed suit and spoke gregariously, and then he whispered. "Yes, we are very close in size. A change of clothes will be appreciated."

Henry looked around to make sure no one was paying

attention to the newcomers. However he still kept his voice low. "Good. I will have my eldest daughter, Lydia, bring them to the barn. I will also send a pot of hot mutton stew with her, enough food for all of you." Henry smiled.

"Ah, yes, a hot meal. We will all be looking forward to that. How much do I owe you for these carrots and the eggs I have here?" Alden held a small wooden box filled to overflowing with a generous bunch of carrots and a half dozen large duck eggs.

"You owe nothing for the work that you and your men are doing. I am the one who owes you a debt that can never be repaid, as do all of your countrymen, yet they will never know. Take what you and your men need. I am honored to help the cause such as I can."

Alden picked up a few more eggs and thanked his friend. He showed Jacob through the rest of the market and into the tiny village.

"The villagers are, for the most part, farmers and sheep herders. A millhouse, a creamery, a cobbler, and a pub make up the total exchange of the village. However, the pub gets the lion's share of the villagers' money." Alden laughed.

Their final stop was the creamery for a liter of goat's milk, after which they started back toward the countryside. Just as they reached the edge of the village, Jacob turned and looked back.

"What is it, Jacob?"

"Nothing, nothing." Jacob answered, but it *was* something. "I thought my brother called to me." Jacob was certain that he had heard his brother call his name from the village. He would not travel to the village again without Auvil.

"Come. Let's carry on to the barn. The men will be wondering about us if we do not hurry along."

Finally, Jacob and Alden reached the barn. As they stood at the barn door, Jacob stopped.

"Do you hear that, Alden?"

"Yes, I hear the sound of our men talking."

"But my men, they are laughing as they talk. It has been a long time since we had any mirth. Hitler has made certain of it. It's good to hear their laughter again."

"They have hope now, Jacob, so they make merry."

"Yes, here we have hope. There is no hope from

where we came. In our ravaged country the children are taught to inform on their parents, and citizens are rewarded for turning their neighbors over to government officials for perceived crimes. Entire families have been sent to the camps or have gone into hiding. Truly Alden our home has been transformed into a place of horror."

"Yes. We shall work together to end that horror, my friend." Alden gave Jacob a strong pat on the back and then slid the barn door open.

"Have we missed the meeting of the minds?" Alden laughed as he addressed the men.

"Not yet. We are just trading tales," Seth offered an explanation for the great deal of levity that he and the men were taking pleasure in.

"We brought food and a promise of a change of clothes." Jacob's men cheered at the good news.

"Jacob, I would like to familiarize you with our laboratory. We will take this food down to the cellar, and then I will show you around."

"Very good, but first I must tell my friends what I have learned today."

"Of course," Alden sat in the straw while Jacob told the others about the village market and the trusted friend Henry. He warned of the Nazi sympathizers and the need to keep to themselves and not venture into town. Jacob would only return to the village with Alden and Auvil. The men agreed then returned to their discussions.

In the cellar, Alden familiarized Jacob with the retort since refinement, the most important process, would be Jacob's first lesson. Alden picked up each bottle and explained the decoction or concoction that filled it. The mixtures were by and large extracts of plants and animal parts. The most precious potions held the basic essence of minerals that had been captured in the distillation process. Now bottled and corked, the potions quite simply sit on the shelves in a state of flux, waiting for their moment to transmute or to merely cure a cough.

Alden turned to face his colleague. Jacob could see the worry in his eyes.

"Jacob I am concerned. You claim that you heard your dead brother call to you when we were leaving the village. I must ask. Do you think you are up to the work that lies before

63

us? Perhaps you need a little more time to grieve. Certainly Seth could step in for you. There's no shame in that."

"I appreciate your concern, Alden, but truly, I am bearing up as I have said and honestly believe my priority is and must be with the living," Jacob replied. "I will grieve my brother when this is done."

"But what about the voice you heard?"

"I believe it was a warning. My brother is still looking after me…but do not worry about it interfering with our work. I will merely take Auvil with me whenever we return to the village, and I suggest that you also take him when you venture out."

"So you believe the ones that have passed to the spirit world can travel here. Is that so, Jacob?"

"I do. I also believe that we can travel in the spirit, but I have not discovered how."

"What makes you think such a thing?"

"Because of the story of our ancestor Jacob and the ladder he saw coming from the heavens and the spirits traveling to Earth from the spirit realm upon that ladder."

"That story speaks only of *spirits* traveling on the

ladder. Tell me why you think it relates to the physical being."

"The story tells of Jacob *wrestling* with a spirit. Do you find that strange?"

"I have never thought of it as strange or otherwise. Please continue Jacob."

"According to what I have been taught a spirit, unlike an angel or a ghost, is not corporal and never has been. It is totally spirit."

"Yes, I believe that also."

"However, Jacob was a man, a man created flesh *and* spirit by The Creator," Jacob continued. "I think when Jacob took hold of the spirit to wrestle him; he must have been in the ladder. Moreover when he was in the ladder he became more spirit than flesh. He, in other words, transmuted. Therefore, Jacob was able to take hold of the spirit and wrestle with him to demand a blessing. The spirit finally blessed him, but the damage Jacob sustained from the fight caused Jacob to walk with a limp from that night on. You see, Alden that is the proof. The spirit damaged Jacob because he was still flesh even though he was in the spirit. However, although Jacobs's flesh was weak, his spirit was strong so he endured to the end. That is why he received his blessing. He endured to the end."

"That is incredible, Jacob. So you are saying that you think it is possible to enter this ladder as flesh!"

"Yes, that is what I think. I also think that there are many of these ladders. I think they are doors to the spirit world."

"I am inclined to agree with you, Jacob."

"I do not imagine that you could disagree. It is a perfectly logical conclusion that I have drawn from the facts as I understand them." Jacob sat on a hard wooden bench pulled off his boot and groaned.

"Are you hurt?"

"I am fine, but I fear that my boots are quite worn," Jacob continued. "Perhaps you have a sheet of old newsprint that I can have to build up the sole of my boot and protect my foot from the hole there within?"

"Certainly, I have a discarded piece of paper here quite handy just perfect for your need. I am curious. Can you tell me what your first question to yourself was? The question that brought you to the amazing hypothesis that you have laid out?"

Jacob finished stuffing his boot with the folded newsprint and jammed his foot into the worn shoe. "To tell you, I must start at the beginning."

"All the better." Alden pulled a stool in front of the bench where Jacob sat and listened to his story.

"When I was a child," Jacob began, "my mother always brought me along to the spring in the field behind our home where she washed the clothes. Each week, she would wash, and I would run and play in the field. It was great fun. Then one day, I happened to catch my smallest toe on a stick. I sat on the ground and bemoaned my aching toe. My toe was no bigger than a field bean, but it had become the source of what I considered an unbearable pain.

"I studied my tiny toe. Then I covered it with my finger. Now I could see only four toes. I thought this is how my foot would look if I had knocked the toe completely off. Then I realized that if I *had* actually knocked my toe off, I would still be me, Jacob Nathaniel Davidson. I then covered all of my toes, and I determined I was still Jacob Davidson.

Amazed, I folded my leg under my haunch and sat on it. Still even without my entire leg, I found that I was still me. Realizing at that moment that I am not any part of my body, I became intent on knowing what exactly I am. I ran to my mother and asked 'What am I, Mother?' She answered, 'You are my precious boy, Jacob.' Of course, I knew that and was slightly disappointed by her answer. It was then that I knew I must discover what I truly am. As a result, I have since searched for my actuality."

"Have you discovered it?"

"Only in part, Alden. Only in part. However, all will be revealed, I am certain."

"We will go to my uncle in the village. He is the cobbler. He will fix your boot. However, now we must boil some carrots and duck eggs. Our men are undoubtedly hungry for their evening meal." The laboratory would now become the hungry men's dining room. The men would rehash the events of the day and then retire to clean dry straw and the warm horse blankets that awaited them.

CHAPTER FOUR

SANDALPHON

November 9, 2014

The emergency room's nurse's station stands like an island in the sea of calamities. Orderlies and aids race gurneys down the halls and along corridors like Roman gladiators with the helpless patients strapped to their speeding chariots. Chest pain sufferers stumble blue-faced through the hospital doors. Wailing rises from treatment areas. Gang members and their rivals sit only a few feet from each other, separated only by curtain walls. They lament brothers that have fallen victim of a drive-by shooting, a knife wound, or some other act of violent aggression that was wielded in retribution for another act of real or imagined aggression.

Mike sidesteps a gurney as it speeds past.

"How 'bout Greek when we get outta here?" Mike whispers to Vicky.

"Papa Louis? Sure, sounds good," Vicky agrees.

They approach the nurses' station just as the desk phone rings.

"Tampa General Hospital, emergency room, nurses' station. No, this is Tampa General Hospital, not Tampa Community Hospital. Yes, you're welcome." The nurse returns the telephone to its receiver. "Can I help you, officer?" Smiling, the nurse appraises Mike while ignoring Vicky. Vicky rolls her eyes and pretends to study her notepad.

Mike, who considers himself a sensitive, caring, twenty-first-century, deadly good-looking Italian man, smiled back.

"Can we see Sister Jane Doe?" he asks.

"Let me check her status. Wait here." Glancing back over her shoulder the nurse smiles at Mike as she enters the curtained room.

"I don't know what you've got Mike, but you should bottle it. You'd make a fortune." Vicky looks up from her notepad just as the nurse walks back over.

"The doctor is in with her now. She hasn't regained consciousness yet," the nurse says.

"Can we speak with the doctor?" Mike asks.

"Just a minute. I'll check." A moment later, the nurse returns and leads Mike and Vicky into the treatment room.

Monitors beep, buzz, and chime a symphony as life-giving fluids drip intravenously. The resident doctor and the chief of staff stand over the unconscious woman.

"Hi, Mike. Are you on this one?" Doctor David Knowles says to his friend and cycling buddy.

"Yeah, me and Vicky. I'd like to finish up and get out of here as soon as I can. What can you tell us, David?" Vicky walks over to try to get a closer look at the woman.

"Not much, I'm afraid. It appears to be an attempted suicide. She has no identification. However, she does have a tattoo on the inside of her forearm. Not something you'd expect a young girl to have. No hearts, flowers, or butterflies—just two letters and a string of numbers. The only word she has spoken is 'Sandalphon.'"

"Well, David, we'll keep in touch. I bet the little *boutana* has half the *cojones* in Tampa under her little nun

71

outfit." Mike swears under his breath as he and Vicky turn to leave.

"And it looks like she's been tortured."

"What?" Mike spins back around to face the doctor.

"By the marks on her wrists and ankles, it appears that she has been bound, very tightly. Someone wasn't playing. She has marks on her shoulders and neck that look to be cigarette burns, and it seems that she's been choked. We have a pretty good idea, but we won't know for sure about everything that has happened to her until she wakes up and we're able to talk to her."

"When she wakes up, give me a call. I want to talk to her as soon as she's able. Vicky, can you get a good picture of her face?"

"Sure thing. Vicky's phone flashed into the unconscious woman's face. Okay, I think I got a pretty good one. I'll get it printed out when we get back to the station."

"Good we'll ask around about her." Mike turns back to David Knowles and takes a card from his shirt pocket. "Call me at this number, David. Tortured… *Mierda*," Mike mumbles as he and Vicky leave the room. Growing up in

72

Tampa, Mike learned to swear fluently in three languages, four if you count English.

Mike and Vicky leave the doctors with their sleeping enigma. As they walk past the nurses' station, the flirtatious nurse looks up from her charts, long enough to bid Mike farewell and flash one more dazzling smile.

Mike takes another calling card from his shirt pocket.

"Will you call me the minute she wakes up?" Mike places the card in the nurse's hand, hesitating a moment as his fingers tips brush hers.

"Oh, I surely will."

"Thanks. I really appreciate that." Mike winks at the nurse and then hurries to catch up to Vicky, who is waiting by the exit.

"Geez, you were laying it on kind of thick back there. Just try to keep your mind on the case, Michael." Vicky scolds.

"Never hurts to be nice." Mike gallantly holds the door for Vicky. She rolls her eyes as she walks through.

Doctor Knowles returns to the woman's bedside. The

chief of staff, Doctor Sam as he is affectionately known as by the hospital staff, stands at the head of the bed, quietly assessing the unconscious young woman.

"'Sandalphon...' I know that word, 'Sandalphon.' Hmm. It'll come to me." Doctor Sam says as he searches his memory.

"I'm sure it will. I don't know what we'll do when you retire. You've got just about everything stored up there." David points to Sam's noggin.

"Not everything, David, but I've seen my share of life, and I think I have a few good years left before I retire." Sam smiles.

"Well, what do you make of this tattoo?" The young resident lifts the woman's arm to study the tattoo one more time.

Doctor Sam looks away. "I've seen tattoos like that, but she's too young."

"It's been a long day. Transfer her to ICU, David. I'll have her blood work sent to my office, and I'll call the monastery before I go home. We'll talk tomorrow."

"Goodnight, Sam."

"Goodnight, David." Doctor Sam walks directly to the nurses' station.

"I want to know the minute that woman wakes up. I'll be in my office for a while. Call me if you need me."

"Yes, Doctor." The nurse's curiosity piques.

Doctor Sam walks to his office and hangs his coat on the hall tree next to his carved mahogany desk. His office is comfortably elegant. The doctor's diploma from Oxford School of Medicine, *Magna Cum Laude*, is the only one of his many accolades that holds a place on his office wall alongside his vast collection of original watercolor art.

"Sandalphon." He shakes his head, repeating the familiar word as he sits at his desk.

Still shaking his head, he rolls the cuff of his crisp, white shirt to his elbow. Stretching his arm across his desk, he studies his own tattoo—two letters and a string of numbers. In 1945 the Allies liberated the Nazi death camps. The hardened battle worn soldiers had come from bloody battlefields where their friends and comrades had suffered and died. These soldiers, with tears in their eyes were the first to look upon a nation's inhumanity. Samuel David Rubinstein was eight years old when a soldier carried him, starving and near death from such a camp.

Doctor Sam buzzes his receptionist.

"Will you get me the number for the Holy Trinity Monastery? Yes, it's in Kumquat, and please ring it through? Thanks, Deloris."

Kumquat, Florida, is a sleepy little township that sits a few miles past the edge of the Tampa city limits, just east of downtown Tampa. The town took its name from the small citrus fruit which grows in abundance there. The townspeople are standoffish, quite backward, and mostly disagreeable.

Doctor Sam was lost in the memories on his arm when the telephone rang.

"Hello, Doctor Rubinstein here."

"Hello, Doctor. I'm the prioress of the Holy Trinity Monastery. Your receptionist said you have a question for me?

Doctor Sam chooses his words as the caller identifies herself. Doctor Sam will not violate his patient's confidentiality, but the young woman's identity must somehow be discovered.

"Yes, Sister, we have a young woman who is unconscious in our ICU. She has no identification, but we think she is possibly one of your sisters. She was found sitting on a park bench here in Tampa. When she was brought into the hospital, she was wearing an outdated habit."

"A habit? You mean a full habit?"

"Yes, Sister, she was wearing a full habit."

"My word, that *is* unusual. We haven't been in full habit since Vatican II changed everything in the sixties. Can you tell me anything else about her?"

"The only word she has spoken is 'Sandalphon.' Does that word mean anything to you, Sister? Can you tell me if there are any sisters unaccounted for or missing from the monastery?"

"None of the sisters who live here are missing, Doctor, and Sandalphon doesn't mean anything to me, although we do have some visitors coming from Europe for our seventy-fifth anniversary celebration. They're due here tomorrow. She may be one of them. Many of the European sisters do still wear the full habit. I'll ask if they are missing anyone from their group in the morning when they arrive."

"Thank you for your time, Sister. Please call if you have any information."

"Of course. Goodbye, Doctor."

"Goodbye." Doctor Sam's eyes fall on his tattoo once again. *"Sandalphon, yes!"* Doctor Sam remembers. He chooses a book from the library table behind his desk.

"Sandalphon, Sandalphon, Sandalphon…" he repeats as he turns the yellowed pages of the ancient book. "There you are! Sandalphon, the spirit on the first rung of Jacob's ladder," he reads out loud. "The guardian of all humans. All right, Sandalphon, you're in charge now. I'm going home!" Doctor Sam speaks to the air as he returns his father's Kabbalah to the table.

Zoe beams every time Mike and Vicky come into Papa Louis. As they take their usual table, Zoe teases the officers.

"Mike, Veekie, so good to see you. Have you two married yet?" Zoe has been trying to push them in the direction of matrimony for years.

"No, Zoe, maybe next time you ask." Mike laughs

nervously. Unflustered, Vicky studies the menu.

Zoe smiles. "Not yet, eh? Such a shame, you two been coming here together for so many years and you, Mike, since you were so young." Zoe puts her hand out even with her shoulder to signify how tall Mike was then.

"Zoe, you're making me feel old now."

"We are only as old as our little finger, Mike." Zoe crooks her little finger and laughs.

No one knows Zoe's age. What is known about Zoe is that for the twenty-five years Papa Louis has been in business, she remains beautiful, gracious, and ever young.

Mike looks up from his Slovaki sandwich just as the Duetzman family filed in—the rapacious daughters and sons of Richard Duetzman and their ill-mannered children, three generations of Tampa's society. Children, grandchildren, nieces, and nephews are all followed by none other than the patriarch himself, Richard Duetzman.

"I'm glad I'm almost finished. I'm about to lose my appetite." Mike glares at the family.

"Just eat, Michael. Ignore him."

"I can't. You know he's gonna come over when he

spots me. What a hypocrite." Mike fumes as he finished his sandwich.

"*Mike*! How ya doin'?" Red Duetzman spots Mike and limps over to the table. "Let me take care of your check. This one's on me for all the good you boys in blue do. Oh, and girls. Excuse me, miss." Red nods condescendingly to Vicky as he takes the bill from the table.

"That's not necessary." Mike snatches the bill from Duetzman's hand.

"How's your brother?"

"Fine."

Mike's radio crackles. "10-91d Bayshore and Bay to Bay." Mike and Vicky hurry to the register.

"I wonder why he limps." Vicky watches as Red makes his way back to his table.

"I heard he got thrown off the roof of a barn by an angry farm hand when he was a kid. It happened in Georgia at a tobacco farm that his family owned. They say the worker's son fell from the hay loft and Red's father wouldn't allow the doctor onto the farm to treat the kid. Supposedly the kid died, and soon after, one of the workers threw Red off the roof. The worker was never seen or heard from again, and Red has limped ever since then. I don't know…that's just the story I heard." Mike shrugs.

"Well my grandmother always said that the fruit doesn't fall far from the tree."

"Yeah, I guess she was right. They're all bad apples, that's for sure, except Victor. Don't know what happened there, but he's really a good guy."

"Why did Red ask about your brother?" Vicky asks as they drove toward the station.

"Nick dated one of his daughters, nothing serious, but it worried the old man. One day, the old guy came to him with his checkbook and asked him what he'd take to disappear from her life. Nick told him to shove his money and dropped his daughter soon after that. Turns out he should have dropped her sooner. She gave him herpes. You know the gift that keeps on giving." Mike is quiet for a moment. "And I don't like Red's pal, Joe Vicente. My dad was working on a case against Vicente when he was killed. I was in high school at football practice when my father was shot. Red's son, Victor, was on the team. We were pretty good friends back then. Victor drove like a wild man, right up to the door of the emergency room. He got me to the hospital in time to say goodbye to my father. I will always be grateful to him for that."

Vicky quietly listened as Michael once again shared his heartrending story.

"Does Victor still live around here?" She asked.

"I haven't heard from him in years. I think he left the Tampa area. He's the only good one in the whole family. I figure he doesn't want to be associated with them."

"Do you want to go by the Bayshore and check out that mess they found? We've got some time before our shift ends."

Mike turns the cruiser and heads toward Bayshore Boulevard, the longest most beautiful stretch of unbroken promenade in the world, according to the Tampa chamber of commerce.

"I know Wallace and Daniels got it, but we can check it out anyway. Bet you the next pizza it's a Santeria sacrifice."

"Okay, you're on."

"It's a dog."

"No way. It's a goat."

Officers Wallace and Daniels argue as they stand in a secluded niche of the Bayshore sidewalk. The bloody carnage of an animal sacrifice lay mutilated at their feet. Unfortunately, ritual sacrifices often litter the longest, most beautiful stretch of unbroken promenade in the world.

"Whatcha got, Wallace?" Mike interrupts.

"It's a goat."

"It's a dog," Daniels insists.

"Well, whatever it is, I just won a pizza."

CHAPTER FIVE

AMICA MIA

Tap...tap...tap...Tap, tap, tap.

Standing in the doorway of Jane Doe's hospital room, Mike watches as an aged nun examines the habit that hangs beside the young woman's bed. The old sister slips her hand into the deep pocket of the habit and withdraws several pieces of broken blackboard chalk. She digs deeper into the pocket and finds an ornate silver rosary worked with amethyst beads.

Tap, tap, tap.

"*Oh, mio Dio. Sei tu, Amica mia.*" The nun crosses herself. "What has happened to you?" she whispers as she stands looking into face of the unconscious young woman. The aged nun turns and hurries from the woman's room.

Mike steps aside to allow her to leave the room. As he

watches the nun makes her way down the hospital corridor, Mike mutters, "Yeah, we all wonder what happened to your friend."

Tap, tap, tap, tap, tap.

Mike's training and his gut tell him that there is something more to this case. There is something more than merely a beaten and tortured woman in a nun outfit—likely another prostitute dressed up for some john's odd amusement, and now the beaten and tortured woman is lying unconscious after an attempted suicide. Mike's gut is never wrong. There is more, but how much more could there be?

Tap, tap, tap, tap.

"Hey, Mike. Here for an update?" Doctor Knowles says as he and Doctor Sam enter the patient's room.

"Yeah. How is she today?"

Tap, tap, tap. Tap, tap, tap.

"Her vitals are good. She could wake up soon." Doctor Knowles makes notes on the patient's chart as he speaks.

"Why hasn't she come around?" Mike asks.

"It's not uncommon for a trauma patient to shut down

85

and remain unresponsive."

"How long usually?"

"It's a measure of stress. It could be a long period, or it could be a short period."

Tap, tap, tap, tap.

"There was an old woman in here when I got here, a nun. Did she say she knows who this Jane Doe is?" Mike continues.

"She's visiting the Holy Trinity Monastery from somewhere in Europe. She said that she doesn't know who the girl is, but the sister did ask if she could come back tonight and give her Holy Communion if she is awake"

Tap, tap.

"She said she doesn't know her, but she wants to come back to give her communion? That's odd." Mike analyzes this bit of new information. Mike's gut is whispering, "*I told you so.*"

"Yeah, that's what she said. We just spoke to her in the hall as she was leaving." Doctor Knowles continues studying his patient's chart.

Tap.

"What's that tapping sound?" Doctor Knowles closes the young woman's chart and looks from side to side. He checks and rechecks each monitor.

Tap, tap, tap, tap, tap.

"That noise is going to drive me crazy. I'll call maintenance. Maybe they can find where it's coming from." David Knowles' eyes dart around the room, searching for the cause of the tapping.

Doctor Sam stands quietly beside the woman's bed. *Tap, tap.* He turns toward the window and opens the mini blinds.

Tap, tap, tap, tap.

"Look. It's a raven. He's tapping on the window." The three men peer through the glass at a large raven.

"It might be her bird. I've heard that ravens can be tamed and that they can even be taught to talk." Mike leans closer to the window. "Pretty bird, Pret-tee burrd," Mike coos through the glass.

"Pretty bird?" Doctor Knowles cannot contain his laughter. The sight of the police officer making 'smoochie' noises at the bird on the other side of the window glass is more than the sleep-deprived resident can seriously process.

Mike clears his throat and straightens up. "I'll come back later."

"David, you should get some sleep," Doctor Sam walks back toward his office.

Doctor Knowles finishes his report and continues his rounds.

Tap, tap, tap.

"I see you, Sandalphon. Is this a trick? English, they were speaking American English. Are they waiting for me to wake up so they can begin their interrogation? I will keep my eyes closed and ears open until I devise a means of escape." The young woman speaks fondly to the only thing familiar to her in this strange and frightening place.

Vicky sits in a corner of the emergency room waiting area. A woman sits next to her, hesitantly answering Vicky's questions. Mike leans against the wall and listens as Vicky talks to one of her "unfortunate ladies of the night."

"I don't want no trouble," Joniqua whispers.

"It looks to me like you've already got you some

trouble." Vicky looks into the woman's bruised face and blackened eyes. "Joniqua, this isn't the first time I've seen you like this. Was it a john?"

"*No.* I told you I'm off the street. I've been off for months, and I'm not goin' back neither." Joniqua was pretty once, but now she is tired, and she looks it. Years of working the streets of Tampa has taken its toll. Joniqua could pass for a good forty-five; she has just turned twenty-seven.

"Looks like you were mixin' it up with Vicente's boys, Joniqua." Standing over Joniqua, Mike takes the picture of Jane Doe from his shirt pocket. "Do you recognize this woman? Is she one of Vicente's girls?" Mike shoves the picture in Joniqua's face.

"Mike, back off." Vicky gave Mike a stern look. Mike backed off. He knew he was in trouble with Vicky.

"I ain't never seen her before, like I said. I don't work for him anymore. I told you. I don't want no trouble. I have nothing more to say." Joniqua turns her face to the window and stares at the cold, dark Tampa Bay.

Vicky walks away in silent anger. She knows Joniqua was going to talk before Mike interrupted her. Mike follows

Vicky to the hospital's courtyard. He is sure that there was more ire to come from his normally mild tempered partner. Vicky is certain that Vicente had something to do with Joniqua's sudden outbreak of bumps and bruises. And certainly might have something to do with Jane Doe's. She has seen other women who had quit Vicente break out with the same symptoms. Vicky has worked for years to gain the trust of the street women. However, without a statement from one of the women, she is getting nowhere fast.

"Don't ever do that again. Joniqua was talking before that Vicente crack. Those women trust me, and they're a link to Vicente, our only link right now. Remember that Mike before you let the chip on your shoulder get in the way of our job."

"I'm sorry. You're right," Mike apologizes, as they buckle into the cruiser and Mike starts the engine.

"You know you have to let go of some of this Vicente stuff if you want to pick up your father's investigation. You have to distance yourself or forget the whole thing. Hear?"

"That's kind of hard to do, Vicky. He had my father murdered, sure as hell." Mike defends himself even though he knows Vicky is right. "Speaking of murder the chief asked me go over to Kumquat after my shift. Looks like some lady got herself murdered in her house last night."

"Don't try to change the subject Mike. Maybe Vicente did have your dad killed. Maybe he didn't. Maybe you're just too close to this case to take it on. You better think about it, Mike."

Joseph Vicente headquarters the southeast crime syndicate from his home on the exclusive Davis Islands. He chose Davis Islands because of the canals that lead into the Gulf of Mexico, allowing easy access to the Tampa seaport's illegal drug trade. Vicente also relies on the Davis Islands' private airport to always insure his fast getaway. Mike hopes to soon take the detective's exam and reopen the investigation of Joseph Vicente, the investigation which cost his father his life.

"10-55. Channel Side Drive," the radio squawks. A body has been discovered on Channel Side.

"10-49. ETA, three minutes," Vicky answers.

There is already a crowd gathering on Channel Side

when Mike and Vicky arrive at the scene.

"We'll probably be here the rest of the day. If you cordon off the area, I'll talk to the guy over there. I'm betting he found the body," Mike says.

"Gang stuff, I'm guessing." Vicky walks to the back of the cruiser and opens the trunk.

"I hope we can get this done quick so I can get back to the hospital. I want to question that old nun who visited Jane Doe this afternoon."

"I thought you said she didn't know Jane Doe." Vicky grabs a roll of crime scene tape.

"No, I said she *claims* she doesn't know her. Therein lies the difference, my good woman."

"So you think she's lying? What makes you think that?"

"I overheard her talking to herself in the woman's hospital room. She called the Jane Doe her friend. Also, she searched the woman's habit, and it looked like she found something then put it back. I'm sure she knows who she is. I just don't know why she's lying."

"Okay, Michael, let's wrap this one up real quick."

Vicky waves the roll of tape in front of Mike's face.

"I get it. Crime scene tape, wrap it up. Everyone's a comedian." Mike is relieved Vicky had called him Michael. All is well.

The drive back to the hospital is a quiet one. The events of the day are being processed, cubby holed, and stored. The information will be retrieved for future reference or will be relived in the throes of a haunting nightmare. A teenage boy has been found lying dead in an alley stripped naked, save one red Nike. Twelve bullets are lodged in the young boy's torso. Another two are in his head. The rats, the roaches, and the homeless who live in the alleys and in the abandoned warehouses are the only witnesses, and none of them are talking.

Hospital visiting hours will soon be over. While Mike parks the cruiser, the old nun leans over the young woman's bed. As she quietly speaks, the woman opens her eyes.

"My name is Sister Theresa Marie. I have been directed to help you."

The young woman listens as the sister speaks. The R's

roll from her tongue. The voice sounds like it belongs to her friend, Theresa Marie, but the aged and wrinkled face is not the face of the woman she knows.

"*You will always find the truth in the eyes.*" Familiar words echo in her memory. She looks into the old woman's sad eyes.

"How can you be the woman I have prayed for these many years? It is impossible." the sister whispers.

Shock and unconsciousness overtake the young woman once again.

Mike hurries to the elevator. He hopes he will get a minute to question the old woman he watched earlier in Sister Jane Doe's room. A minute to question the nun is all he needs. That is all it will take. Then he will know for sure if she is lying.

Mike and Vicky step off the elevator; they can see a commotion at the nurses' station. Doctor Knowles runs past them.

"What's going on?" Mike hurries to catch up with Knowles.

"It's Jane Doe. Looks like she's in shock. Wait here." He shakes his head. "No, go talk to that nun in the ICU lounge."

Mike and Vicky make their way to the ICU lounge. The sister is sitting quietly twisting her rosary ring.

"I'll take this one, if you want. You can just sit and watch me do all the work."

"Go ahead. I could get used to this." Vicky laughs as Mike walked over and sat next to Sister Theresa Marie.

"*Buonasera.*"

"I speak English," the sister says.

"My name's Mike De Augustino. I'd like to ask you some questions about the young woman you visited today."

"Yes, I understand," Sister Theresa Marie speaks quietly.

"Do you know her?" Mike continues.

"She bears a strong resemblance to someone I knew many years ago, but of course it cannot be her. I believe that person to be dead for more than sixty years."

"If you don't know her, then why did you call her your friend when you were here earlier? Why did you offer to come back to give her Holy Communion?"

"I am a sister of the Order of Saint Benedict. I offer my friendship and prayers to all who are in need."

"Sister, this woman is in serious condition," Mike urged. "We don't know who she is or who her family is. If you really want to help your friend, you must tell us anything you know about her."

Sister Theresa Marie looks into Mike's face. "There is nothing I can tell you. I am sorry, but I cannot help you. I must return to the Holy Trinity. It's getting late."

"How old do you think she is?" Vicky whispers as the old nun slowly made her way down the corridor.

"Older than God's shoelaces."

"Hush, Michael. She'll hear you."

"She's around the corner. She can't hear me. She probably doesn't even remember me."

"You're kidding yourself, Michael. She's sharp."

"Yeah damn it, she is. Well, I know she's lying."

"Lying? Think about it. She's not lying. She would have had to actually answer your questions to do that. How can she be lying?" Vicky laughs.

"C'mon, let's go." Mike heads toward the commotion.

"What happened here tonight?" Mike asks Doctor Knowles.

"All we know is that she went into shock after the old sister came back to visit her. She's stable now, but the next seventy-two hours are going to be crucial. It's strange though. The monitors are showing she's not responding to anything, just that bird that keeps tapping at the window."

"She's so young, poor girl, and she's been so badly treated," Vicky says.

"Calm down, Vic. You can't save all the ladies of the night."

"She's not a prostitute," Doctor Knowles interrupts.

"She's not?" Mike is strangely disappointed and relieved.

"We examined her for rape when she first came in, and the results from the exam showed that this woman has no signs that she's sexually active so I think we can rule out your little nun *boutana* theory. Sorry, Mike, check back in a day or two. Maybe you can come up with a better theory by then." Doctor Knowles sits in the chair beside the woman's bed.

"I'm going to take my break in here. She needs the company." David Knowles yawns.

Tap, tap, tap.

Jane Doe moans.

"Don't worry, bird buddy. I'll take good care of her."

Jane Doe sleeps. Her dreams bring forth sorrowful moans. However, her cries are hopeless, not one familiar soul comforts her. She is alone. Nothing is recognizable, save for her dreams.

CHAPTER SIX

THE GROTTO

Tap, tap, tap.

"Come in." Miriam wiped the tears from her eyes as the heavy wooden door to her convent room opened. A tiny woman entered the room.

"My name is Sister Theresa Marie. I have been directed to help you." Sister Theresa Marie's German was influenced by an Italian accent. The young sister stood a little more than a meter and a half tall. Her round dark eyes peered from behind gold-rimmed glasses. Her olive complexion was accentuated by the stark white linen coif that framed her face and the contrast of the black wool veil that hung past her shoulders. Theresa Marie held a large package neatly wrapped in brown paper. "This is for you. It is a habit. I made it for you." Theresa Marie smiled warmly.

"Thank you." Miriam took the package. "What do you mean 'directed to help me?'"

"Mother Mary Gertrude, our superior, has charged me with helping you. Besides me, Mother Mary Gertrude, and the mother superior at the monastery in Düsseldorf, no one knows about you and your father. We will be the only people who know your secret. You will be safe here. Do not worry. But now, you must put the habit on. I will take your clothes to the furnace." Sister Theresa Marie spoke quietly.

"What about the other sisters? What will they think?" Miriam asked as she undressed.

"We are under a vow of obedience to the mother superior. No one will question her." Sister Theresa Marie neatly folded Miriam's clothes and wrapped them in the brown paper.

"I understand. I am also under a vow. I gave an oath to God that I will stay here and accept my existence, whatever it may be. I am bound to that oath now, until I marry." Miriam hung her head and averted her eyes. What will the mother superior tell the sisters?" Miriam lifted her head took a deep breath and forced a smile.

"Mother Mary Gertrude has told our community that you are her niece from Düsseldorf and that your family has died in a house fire. She said that you came from our sister convent for a time of seclusion and recollection. That means you will be away from the others and in silence. No one will talk to you or look at you. Since the other sisters will not be paying attention to your business, you will have time to learn how to act like a sister. After I have taught you what you need to know to pass as one of us, Mother Gertrude will announce to our community that you have broken your silence. She will also tell them that you have asked to be allowed to enter our community. The sisters will be thrilled." Sister Theresa Marie smiled as Miriam struggled with the habit.

"Why do you call the prioress Mary Gertrude? Her name is Emma Herder. She and her brother, Wilhelm, are friends of my father and uncle." Miriam struggled with the yards of dark material. Sister Theresa Marie helped her fidget with it until it was arranged properly.

"When we become sisters, we take the name of a saint, and we take the name Mary for the Blessed Mother of

Christ. So many questions, you don't have to learn everything your first night." She stepped back and looked at Miriam. "Good, it fits. I had to guess at the length, but it looks good. Well, now you look like one of us, *Buona*."

"My mother was Italian," Miriam answered in flawless Italian.

"Mother Gertrude told me that beside German you speak Italian and English. How did you learn English?" Sister Theresa Marie smiled.

"My mother taught me and my father. Her family traveled throughout Europe and England. They spoke many languages and dialects. I learned Italian and English before she died."

"Where is your mother's family now?"

"Switzerland."

"Good. It is safe there. I am from a small town on the Italian-Swiss border called Terre Rouge." Sister Theresa Marie's smile widened as she spoke her native language.

"Terre Rouge, that means 'red earth.' It must be close to the mountains?"

"My, you are clever. It is."

"Why are you here? Was there no monastery for you in your town?" Miriam looked into the sister's sad eyes.

"There was only a small convent. We were a very poor little town. There were very few sisters, so we were all reassigned to larger monasteries. This is where I was sent. That was seven years ago. I was sixteen years old."

"I am sixteen years old, but only two weeks from now, I will be seventeen. My father will come for me before then."

"Miriam, it may be a long time before your father is able to come back for you," the sister conceded. "I will teach you so you can appear as one of us until he does come for you. Do you understand how important it is that everyone believes you are a sister?"

Miriam thoughts raced back to the night that her father found her reading his journal. She was afraid he would be angry.

"I should not have read your journal, Father," she had said. "But I have learned much. However, I know that now I have to accept the result."

"Yes, Daughter, now you must accept the result. You

have gained knowledge, and with knowledge there must

be understanding."

"Will it be difficult, Father, the result?"

"Yes, it will be difficult. However, you have set in

place a strength that will sustain you."

"I understand," Miriam answered.

"Good, it is almost time for vespers. I will be back soon with your dinner. We will talk more then." Sister Theresa Marie turned back before she opened the door. "Oh, and Mother Gertrude suggested that we speak only Italian while I am teaching you."

"Why not English?" Miriam asked.

"My English is poor, but with your help I shall improve. Some of the sisters speak a little English. We are the only two who speak Italian." The sister's smile widened.

Miriam smiled in return. "My English is certainly not perfect either."

"Your English is fine, so you will be the English teacher. Good luck." Sister Theresa Marie chuckled as she turned to leave Miriam's room.

"Wait. What?" Miriam tripped on the generous black

fabric as she hurried to the door.

Sister Theresa Marie peeked around the door and whispered, "I am late for vespers. I will be back soon. Practice walking."

"Practice walking? I have been walking for sixteen years. Now I have to practice?" Miriam grumbled as she tripped once again on the abundance of material that draped her small frame. She maneuvered around her tiny room, trying to mimic the ethereal walk of Mother Gertrude and Sister Theresa Marie.

"This is going to take a lot of practice," Miriam spoke to the ceiling as she fell onto the cot, which along with a Lilliputian bureau, a straight-backed chair, and a small writing table, graced her new living accommodations

"Oi." Miriam closed her eyes. She was tired, but sleep would not come. Instead of sleep, she watched as cheerless images projected themselves onto the deep sepia of her closed eyes.

Tap, tap, tap.

"Come in."

"I have brought you a dinner tray and a few cookies

for later." Sister Theresa Marie set the tray on the writing table. She sat on the edge of Miriam's cot and nibbled on a cookie she took from her deep pocket.

"Thank you." Miriam was not sure what she was being served, but she was hungry. She decided it was stew and did not ask particulars.

"That was very good. Thank you." Miriam studied her dinner tray. The rosebud and the vase were the only things left uneaten.

"The rose is beautiful. It reminds me of my mother. She loved flowers, especially roses."

"I thought you might like one for your room." Sister Theresa Marie's smile came easily, but did not light her eyes. Miriam searched Theresa Marie's sad eyes. Although her sadness was intense, it had not touched her soul.

"I know you said that I am supposed to be in seclusion, but will I be allowed to go outside? I would love to see the rose garden."

"Of course you may go outside. Tomorrow I will take you to the grotto. It is a private garden. We go there for quiet reflection. No one will bother you there."

"Thank you, Sister. You are very kind."

"Please, call me Theresa."

"All right, Theresa. Thank you."

"I have one more thing for you." Sister Theresa Marie withdrew her hand from her pocket and hesitantly placed a silver rosary worked with amethyst beads in Miriam's hand. "This was mine when I was a young girl, it means a lot to me. I am sorry, Miriam. I know this is not part of what you believe, but you must learn to pray like a sister."

Miriam looked in horror at the image of a crucified man. She had never touched a graven image, much less prayed to one. Now with everything else, she would be unclean. A cry lumped in her throat. Tears welled in her eyes, but did not fall.

"I am sorry. I am so sorry, Miriam." Sister Theresa Marie wrapped her arms around Miriam.

"The days of sorrow shall renew themselves." As a storm threatened, Miriam comforted Sister Theresa Marie with her father's words.

Miraculously, the dawn broke, turning the sky from the dark thunderous heavens of the night into the radiant firmament of morning. The world was washed fresh by the storm that had raged during the night. Miriam had been up for hours. From her window, she could see the courtyard beyond the iron gate and the stonewall that secluded the monastery. Two sisters stood at the gate as children filed through with their books in hand; ready to face another day of academia.

Tap, tap, tap.

"Come in," Miriam welcomed Sister Theresa Marie into her room again.

"Are you hungry? I have brought you breakfast." Sister Theresa Marie put the tray on the writing table and uncovered Miriam's breakfast of fruit, cheese, bread, and hot tea.

"Thank you, Sister. It looks wonderful."

"Theresa, remember? Most of the sisters will want you to call them by their name. Some of the sisters are a little hard to get along with and will be more formal." Sister Theresa Marie began the day's instruction. "It is good to have someone to speak Italian with. I have missed my home and my language since I have been here," Sister Theresa Marie admitted to Miriam.

"This is a wonderful breakfast. This cheese is very good. Where does it come from?"

"We make it here. It *is* very good. We even make enough to sell. We sell some of our produce and dairy at the market it brings in a little money to the house.

"Miriam, last night I explained to you why we call your father's friend Gertrude instead of Emma. Do you remember?" Sister Theresa Marie began.

"Yes, I remember."

"Now, you must have a new name. Mother Gertrude has chosen Mary Katherine. Saint Katherine is the protector of young women and guards against being burned, and of course, Mary is the name of the Blessed Mother of Christ.

"I understand." Miriam swallowed the lump that welled again in her throat. "Will you take me to the grotto this morning?" Miriam put her unfinished breakfast aside.

"Yes, but there are a few more things to do before we go out. You must learn what I am going to tell you. Do not write it down. Memorize it! Your given name is Kristen Herder. You are eighteen years old. You are Mother

Gertrude's niece from Düsseldorf, the daughter of her brother, Elmer, and his wife, Hilda. Your parents were killed three months ago in a house fire. You have come here from our sister convent there in Düsseldorf, where you have recently taken your vows as a sister. You are under a special dispensation for a time of seclusion. You have no family other than Mother Gertrude and her brother Wilhelm."

"Eighteen? Who's going to believe that?" Miriam forced a smile.

"It is difficult to judge a sister's age because we are so covered by the habit. A sister's weight can be illusive too." Sister Theresa Marie giggled at her own joke.

Miriam mumbled the facts of her invented life as she followed Sister Theresa Marie through the corridors of the monastery, down the stairs, and past the courtyard. Finally, they reached the grotto, a garden with such a heavy canopy of trees that it seemed cave like.

A large rock sat in the middle of the clearing, worn smooth from years of being sat upon in quiet contemplation.

"Here we are," Sister Theresa Marie said.

"It is so quiet here." Miriam felt the need to whisper,

so as not to break the grotto's silent spell.

"You may come here to be alone. No one will come into the clearing if they see you are here." Sister Theresa Marie left Miriam quietly sitting on the smooth rock. As the morning sun fell through the trees, Miriam listened to the rustle of the leaves. To Miriam's ears, the songs of the birds were sad laments that wafted from somewhere beyond the trees. Miriam sat in the grotto in silence save for the deafening sound of her heart breaking. As she sat wondering how she would ever bear her life, a raven landed at her side. Startled, Miriam jumped to her feet, but the raven stood where it had landed. Miriam returned to her seat and turned toward the large bird.

"You are a pretty one." Miriam leaned closer to the bird. The raven did not move. Miriam bent slightly forward to see the shiny object it held in its beak. "What do you have?"

The raven dropped his prize, a small silver vial at Miriam's feet. Miriam studied the vial.

"The essence," she whispered and held tightly to the vial. The raven moved toward her, she could see a band encircling the bird's leg. She scooped the bird into her hands and examined the band. A woman's wedding ring had been placed on the bird's leg. Miriam removed the ring. Engraved on the front in Hebrew letters was the inscription "I am my beloveds."

"Thank you." Miriam slipped the treasures into the pocket of her habit.

"Hello!" A voice came from the edge of the grotto. "Is that your bird?"

Miriam shaded her eyes against the glare of the morning sun. She looked in the direction of the small voice.

"Who is there?" Miriam called out.

"Stephen." A young boy stepped from the shadows. "My name's Stephen. I always come here at recess. I am sorry, Sister. I guess I should not have disturbed you. But I saw you, and I wanted to see your bird. He sure is big!" Stephen hesitantly advanced. "Is he tame? What is his name? What is your name?" Stephen's cherub-like face shone, and his blue eyes danced.

"My name is Sister Mary Katherine." Miriam nervously tried her new name. "The bird's name is umm Sandalphon." *"That was not too bad. He believed me. But he is probably only eleven or twelve years old. Well, it is a start,*" Miriam thought.

"Sandalphon, good name. I guess most people would have named him Blackie." Stephen squatted to have a closer look at the bird.

Miriam laughed at Stephen's assessment of most people's idea of a creative epithet. The tolling school bell brought Stephen to his feet.

"I have to go back to class now. I will see you tomorrow, if that is okay." Stephen called as he raced back to his studies.

"That would be nice, Stephen," Miriam called back.

Miriam silently walked back to the monastery, ever aware of the large black bird that flew above her. Sister Theresa Marie met Miriam at the monastery door.

"I am on my way to chapel. I will see you after lunch." Theresa Marie hurried along.

Miriam was hungry by the time Theresa Marie brought her lunch.

"Sorry, we had leftovers," she said.

"Thank you, Theresa. It looks good." Miriam sat at

her writing table, prepared to enjoy her lunch. "Yesterday, you said my job would be the English teacher. What did you mean?"

"All of the sisters have a job. Some of the sisters work in the garden, some keep the house, some have missions outside of the monastery, and some are teachers. Since you have knowledge of English, you will be the English teacher in the convent school."

"What is your job, Theresa?"

"I am the mistress of the archives. Also I keep the daily records."

"Records?"

"Yes, a detailed record is kept of each sister from the time she enters the convent until the day she dies."

"Will a record be kept of me?"

"Mother Gertrude and I have already created your records. As mistress of the archives, I am also in charge of preserving the religious icons. While you are learning, you can help me. Can you use a typewriter?"

"I was just learning when I came here. There was only one typewriter in our class, so we all had to take turns."

"You will learn quickly while helping me with the information in the archives." Sister Theresa Marie's calm manner put Miriam at ease.

"I have not practiced my typing as much as I should."

"Do not worry. I will give you plenty of practice. Typing is something that you will always be able to use, and I can really use the help." Sister Theresa Marie walked to the heavy door, and then turned back to Miriam.

"It is nice to have you here, Miriam. It is like having my little sister here. I did not realize how much I miss my home and my language until now. Thank you, Miriam." Sister Theresa Marie gave Miriam a quick hug before she left the room.

The weeks trudged along for Miriam. Although Sister Theresa Marie has shown her immense kindness and patience, much more than Miriam had expected, Stephen and Sandalphon's antics are her only cheer. However, Miriam would keep the promise that she swore to her father. She would go on, she would force a smile, and she would continue to live as one of the sisters. She would learn the sister's ways, pray their prayers, and then when her father returned for her, she would thank The One in heaven for secreting her in this unlikely crevasse.

"Open your hand and close your eyes and I will give something to make you wise." Stephen recited the children's singsong verse as he approached Sister Mary Katherine in the grotto.

"What are you up to?" Sister Mary Katherine asked as Stephen stood in front of her with his hands hidden behind his back.

"Open your hand and close your eyes. It is a surprise, Sister," Stephen insisted.

"Okay, but I hope this is not something crawly." Mary Katherine closed her eyes and held out her open hand. She felt Stephen place something it.

"You can open your eyes now." Stephen giggled.

"Stephen, what a lovely gift!" Sister Mary Katherine was surprised to see a chocolate candy beautifully wrapped in shiny, colored foil.

"My mother sends them to me. She is a confectioner." Stephan sat on the ground next to Sister Mary Katherine and opened his candy.

"Does she have a shop in town?" Sister Mary Katherine asked.

"No, her shop is in Düsseldorf."

"Düsseldorf?" Sister Mary Katherine thought about the city that is contrived to be her home—a city she had never seen.

"Yes, that is where I am from. I helped my mother in her shop before I came here to the monastery's school."

"Düsseldorf. Will you tell me about it?" Sister Mary Katherine thought it could not hurt to borrow some of Stephens's memories from his home.

Stephen beamed as he spoke of his home, his mother, her candy shop, and his desire to become a priest.

"I'm an altar boy now, but Father Ignatius says I can start clerical work soon to prepare for the priesthood… Hey, he took my foil!" Stephen jumped to his feet, pretending to be annoyed at Sandalphon, who had taken the piece of shiny foil from his lap.

"That is what ravens do. My father had a raven when he was a boy that brought him every shiny thing that he found," Sister Mary Katherine said as Sandalphon dropped the foil into her outstretched hand.

"Then I guess your father was foil rich."

"Yes, I guess he was." Sister Mary Katherine smiled.

CHAPTER SEVEN

THE GIFT

Tap. Tap. Tap.

Sister Mary Katherine tapped the ruler on her desk to gain the class's attention. "Good morning, children."

"Good morning, Sister Mary Katherine." The children stood next to their desks and greeted her with the first English phrase they had learned. In three months of study, the students had learned enough English to confound completely anyone they might try to communicate with.

Sister Mary Katherine turned to the chalkboard and picked up a fresh piece of chalk. "Today is December 20, 1939." She spoke the words in English as she printed them across the chalkboard. As she wrote, a paper airplane sailed across the classroom, crashing into the chalkboard.

Sister Mary Katherine dropped the chalk into her deep pocket and turned to face her class as they disintegrated into giggles.

"Airplane." Sister Mary Katherine held the object of hilarity in the air. She turned back to the chalkboard and picked up a piece of fresh chalk. Sister Mary Katherine wrote the word in large letters across the chalkboard.

"Airplane. Repeat after me," Sister Mary Katherine sailed the paper airplane across the room and continued her lessons. After class, Stephen came to Mary Katherine's desk.

"I will come after school and clean the board and erasers if you like, Sister." Stephen was always eager to please.

"That would be nice. Thank you, Stephen." Sister Mary Katherine was preoccupied with grading the stacks of students' papers that lay on her desk. She looked up from her desk to find Stephen studying her. "Yes, dear, is there something else?"

"You are not like the other sisters."

"What? Why do you say that?" Sister Mary Katherine sputtered.

"Well, most of the other sisters would have been angry about the airplane, but you were not angry. You used it to teach us."

"Stephen, we must always learn from our mistakes, or our destiny will be to repeat them." The words of her father's instruction echoed in her ears.

"I hope I will be as good a priest as you are a sister."

"I am sure you will be a wonderful priest."

"I will come back right after school. I have to hurry now to boys' choir practice for the holidays. See you later, Sister." Stephen called.

Sister Mary Katherine watched her precious cherub turn into an impish little boy as he ran to catch his classmates.

Tap, tap, tap, tap, tap.

Mary Katherine's fingers flew across the typewriter's keyboard.

Tap, tap, tap.

"Your boyfriend is on the sill, Mary Katherine." Theresa Marie opened the window of her archives office and allowed Sandalphon to step in.

"Sandalphon. Yes, he is my boyfriend" Mary Katherine laughed. "I think I shall marry him. Then he will release me from my vow, and we will fly away together."

"Oh, no, Mary Katherine, you will not. I will not allow you to fly away from me."

"Do not fear, Theresa Marie. Alas, I have no wings nor can I fly."

"Sandalphon has brought you something." Theresa Marie studied the shiny foil the bird held in his beak.

"It is probably a note from Stephen." Mary Katherine stopped typing and turned toward the window.

"A note?"

"Yes, one day while we were in the grotto, I told Stephen that ravens will bring any shiny thing they find to their person. After that, he started writing notes to me, wrapped in candy foil."

"That is clever of him. Oh yes, and you too, Sandalphon." Theresa Marie stroked Sandalphon's broad chest. As Mary Katherine and Theresa Marie stood at the open window, they could hear angry voices from the office next door. The two young nuns listened quietly as the men argued.

"You know I have finished construction of the Holy Trinity Monastery. Karl, come to the States with me. It will not be good for you to remain here."

"The Holy Trinity? I know that you finished it years ago, and I am sure Mother *thinks* she knows where all of her aristocratic money has gone."

"What are you saying, Karl?" Klaus roared.

"Do you think that I do not know, Klaus? You must think me a complete imbecile. I have access to Mother's accounts, and I have seen them dwindle considerably by your signature. You have misappropriated the lion's share of our family fortune, and yet Mother holds you in high regard while I have always been nothing more than an encumbrance."

"I do not think you an imbecile. No, you are more than an imbecile, Karl. You are a fool and an imbecile. I have enough for all of us in America. Come with me to the States. Mother has finally agreed to leave Düsseldorf. Klaus sighed. "Karl, leave your past, start anew in America as I have. Come with us when we leave. We will be sailing for the States in two days. Travel to Europe from the States is becoming more difficult, so I will not be able to come here again for a long while

Father Ignatius hissed, "Klaus, you really should call me Father."

"I see you are determined to have your way as always, Karl." Klaus Duetzman ignored his brother's request. He had been ignoring his younger brother since the day he was born. Almost fifteen years Karl's senior, the responsibility of keeping the family fell to Klaus upon the premature death of their father. Young Klaus had little time and even less patience for Karl, the hellion of a child, and now no patience at all for Karl, the malignant young man. Klaus turned his back to his brother. He would not speak to him again about coming to America.

Fourteen-year-old Richard Duetzman sat awkwardly in the corner of his uncle's office. He had learned very little of the German language that his father and uncle spoke, but he knew they were arguing again. Richard was sorry when his father and uncle argue. Richard loved his uncle, and his father was…his father.

Richard's father had not taught him to speak German and was unable to teach him any social graces or proper human interaction of any sort. However, he had learned, under his father's tutelage, to straighten ten penny nails and that Jews were less than human. They were responsible for most, if not all, of the problems of the world; worst of all, they were the Christ killers.

"I am offering mass at the monastery this evening. I must prepare. Will you and Richard be at mass, Klaus?"

"Yes, we will be there."

Father Ignatius turned his attention to his young nephew. "Red, tomorrow when the schoolchildren play in the courtyard, you may join them. A young sister from Düsseldorf who speaks English will be out with the children. You might enjoy talking with her."

"All the sisters look alike. I wouldn't know her from any other sister," Richard whined.

"You will know this sister. She and her raven will be playing tag with the children in the yard."

"Tag? How can a bird play tag?"

125

Father Ignatius rumpled Richard's bright red hair. "I think you will have to see that for yourself, Richard."

"Hey, stop it. I'm not a little kid anymore, you know."

"No, you're not. I miss that little boy."

A light snow had fallen during the night, coating the ground with white. Young Richard Duetzman stepped out of the warmth of his room and grumbled. "Snow! I hate this stuff! Glad there's no snow in Florida." He could hear the sounds of the children playing. He trudged toward the schoolyard.

"I can't wait to get home and see Mother." Even though Richard enjoyed the company of his Uncle Karl, no one could take the place of his mother. His mother made the hours he had to spend with his father seem a bit more tolerable.

"Straighten those nails, boy. Do I have to show you again? Can you ever learn? Mama's boy, that's all you are. You are a good-for-nothing mama's boy." Richard mocked his father as he walked, as he often did. He could feel the power behind his father's words lessen with each one he repeated aloud.

Richard followed the sound of children playing as he made his way to the schoolyard. In the yard, screams of laughter rang out. The children ran and jumped into the air, trying to tag a large raven that taunted them as it flew only inches from their reach. A young nun stood laughing as she watched the children's antics.

"That must be the sister from Düsseldorf," Richard grumbled as he approached Sister Mary Katherine. As he drew nearer, Sandalphon swooped down, causing Richard to lose his balance and tumble into the soft snow.

The children continued their game, laughing all the more at the added bonus of seeing someone fall in the soft snow.

"What's so funny?" Richard's green eyes flashed, and his temper flared.

"Let me help you, young man." Sister Mary Katherine offered her hand to Richard.

"Naw, I can get up. I don't need help." Richard refused the sister's hand but slipped backward twice before finally making it to his feet.

"Well, good morning, young man. I am Sister Mary Katherine. The children should not have laughed at your misfortune. I will speak to them about this matter."

"Just forget it." He brushed the snow from his pants.

"You are an American, correct?"

"Yes, I'm from Florida. My name is Richard Duetzman, but everyone calls me Red. I'm not used to the snow. I guess that's the problem."

"You are a long distance from home. What has brought you here?"

"My father and I come almost every year to visit my uncle, Father Ignatius, and my grandmother who lives in Düsseldorf."

"Oh?"

"My uncle said you are from Düsseldorf. What part?"

"*Children*, it's time to go back to class. Richard… Red, it has been nice to meet you, but I must go now. I hope you have a nice visit and a safe trip home." Sister Mary Katherine gathered the children and hurried them back into the classroom before Richard could bid his farewell.

"What an odd duck," Richard said to himself as he

made his way back to the guest quarters.

"Richard, did you go out to the school yard today?" Richard did not reply. He laid a gift next to Father Ignatius's plate. Richard hoped his uncle would like what he had brought him. He had thought long and hard about an appropriate gift for the priest. He had finally settled on the gold bookmark. Richard even spent the extra fifty cents to have it engraved with "To Father Ignatius, Love, Richard."

Father Ignatius picked the gift up and studied it. "Oh, is this for me, Red?" Ignatius pretended to be surprised although Richard brought a gift each time he visited.

"Yes. Open it." Upon Richard's eager words, Ignatius ripped open the gift. He smiled as he saw his present."A bookmark and it is engraved! Thank you, Red."

Richard beamed. "You're welcome."

"Richard! I believe your uncle asked you a question that you rudely ignored," Klaus scolded.

"I asked you if you went out to play today. Did you?" Ignatius said.

"Yeah, I went out," Richard snarled, as he pushed his

food around on his plate.

"Did you get a chance to chase the raven?"

"*No*, that stupid bird knocked me down. Then the dumb kids laughed at me. When I asked the sister about where she lived in Düsseldorf, she took off like her hair was on fire."

Father Ignatius waited until Richard took his next gulp of water before speaking. "Her family was killed in a house fire." Water and uncontrolled laughter spewed from Richard's mouth.

"I guess their hair was on fire." Richard fell from his dining chair and rolled on the floor in throes of exaggerated laughter.

"That's enough, boy. I would like to enjoy the rest of my dinner." Klaus glared at Richard and then his brother. Karl had not been a good influence on his son.

Father Ignatius smiled.

Sister Mary Katherine sat in the grotto with Sandalphon as he preened his feathers, which shined iridescent in the warm spring sun. "The best part of spring is that it comes right after winter." Sister Mary Katherine smiled into the face of the sun. She looked down. "I think you missed a spot, Sandalphon." Sister Mary Katherine crooked her finger and scratched the bird's large black head.

"Good morning, Sister." Stephen had found Sister Mary Katherine and Sandalphon in the grotto.

"Good morning, Stephen. Soon, it will be Easter. Are you enjoying the Holy Days?"

"I suppose so."

"You suppose so? What does that mean? The rest of the children are all happy to be excused from class. What is the matter?" Stephen slumped down beside Sister Mary Katherine. She ruffled his blond curls.

"I still have my altar duties and clerical studies." Stephen crossed his arms over his chest.

"Stephen, what is wrong? Is something bothering you?"

"No, Sister, I will be all right." Stephen dropped his head. His tears fell into the grotto's deep carpet of leaves and moss.

"Come here." Sister Mary Katherine pulled Stephen

131

to herself. She held him as he cried. "Stephen, I will always help you if I can. Do you know that?"

"Yes, Sister. I know." Stephen pulled away and forced a smile. He stuffed his hand in his pocket. "Look, Sister, my mother sent us a holiday treat." Stephen produced two large chocolate bars.

"It is so nice of your mother to remember me. I think these candies are the most beautiful she has sent." Sister Mary Katherine admired the gold foil. The wrapper was delicately embossed with bouquets of pastel spring flowers.

"I will save mine. I think I will just look at it for a while." Stephen studied his candy. His eyes welled again with tears.

"Stephen, tell me what's wrong."

"Oh, Sister, I want to be a priest more than anything. It is all I have ever wanted. But I cannot." Stephen began to cry again.

"Stephen, you should speak to Father. I am sure he will help you."

"No, not Father Ignatius! He…" Stephen was suddenly quiet.

"What about Father?" As Sister Mary Katherine searched Stephen's eyes his tremendous sadness overcame her.

While the shadows lengthened in the grotto, and the sun set, Sister Mary Katherine read the sorrow in Stephen's eyes, the sorrow that had touched Stephens' very soul. As the months passed and spring gave way to summer, Stephen became increasingly distant. He no longer came to the grotto to find Sister Mary Katherine and Sandalphon.

CHAPTER EIGHT

ABSOLUTION

"Bless me, Father, for I have sinned," the man slurred.

Father Ignatius waited, but the man did not continue. He merely sat in the confessional and quietly sobbed.

"How long has it been since your last confession?" Father Ignatius asked, although he did not care how long it had been or if, in fact, the man had ever been to confessions. Nor did he care that the man reeked of alcohol and women.

"I don't know. A year or two? Maybe more." The man belched loudly.

"Why have you come, my son?"

"I'm drunk."

"Have you come to the house of God to seek forgiveness for the sin of drunkenness?"

"Drunkenness? If that were all I am guilty of, I would be at the beer garden now with a woman on each knee," the man sneered.

"God will also forgive the sin of lust."

"Lust, ha. That is a very bad sin, Father." The man laughed bitterly.

"Confess your sin, and the Father will forgive you." Father Ignatius was becoming annoyed.

"There is no forgiveness. Not for me." The man leaned his head against the heavy screen that separated the priest and the parishioner.

"Unless you confess your sins, there is no forgiveness. Only with confession will there be forgiveness and peace."

The man's quiet sobbing rose to a loud wail as the man broke under his burden.

"Father, I have been drunk for almost two years now. It is the only way I am able to live with what I have done."

"Continue, my son."

"At first, the drinking helped, but now there is not enough beer in all of Germany to drown the cries and pleading," the man said.

"What cries, my son?"

"November ninth of thirty-eight. I was there...they call it *Kristallnacht*, the night of the broken glass."

"*Kristallnacht*?" Father Ignatius' heart skipped a beat. He leaned on his hand to partially cover his face With his ear pressed to the screen Ignatius listened intently determined to extract the specifics from this tortured soul.

"Yes, it was in a small town in the countryside. We came through on motorcycles. We smashed up the town. There was a woman hiding in an alley. We beat the man she was with, and then, we went after her. We were like savages, like wild animals. We were Hitler's youth league, the master race, showing our superiority over a crying, helpless woman. We ignored her pleas. When it was my turn to have her, she was badly hurt. As she lay beneath me, dying, she looked into my eyes and said, 'We are going to have a baby, Jacob.' By the time we were finished with her, the poor woman was out of her mind. She thought I was her husband, I can only imagine. When I reported to my captain that the woman was dead and that she had been with child, he laughed and said, 'This is not a bad thing. Now we have rid the world of two

136

Jews instead of only one.' Father, I hear her cries every day. Please help me." The man held his head in his hands and sobbed.

"Do you have remorse for what you have done, my son?"

"Yes, Father, but remorse will not restore that woman."

"If you are truly remorseful, you must make an act of contrition." Father Ignatius tried to see the face of the man who sat on the other side of the heavy screen that separated them in the confessional. "You must say three Hail Mary's for the purity of the Blessed Mother and ten Our Father's for the sanctity of the trinity. Then, you may go, and you are forgiven."

"Is that the worth of that woman's life?"

"God forgives those who repent, my son. Before you go will you tell me the name of that heartless captain? So I can pray for his immortal soul."

"Yes, Father. I will never forget him. His name is Karl Duetzman."

"So he remembers me," Father Ignatius whispered as

he watched the man stagger through the chapel doors.

The summer breeze found its way through Sister Mary Katherine's open window. This particular evening, the sky was spectacular. In her darkened room, as she watched the stars, it seemed like a lifetime since she had shared the summer sky with her father.

"You are capable of doing whatever you wish," he had told her as they sat gazing into the starry night.

"I wish I could dance on the stars. Can I even do that, Father?" she had asked.

"Yes, child, you can even do that."

The stars seemed so close that Sister Mary Katherine thought that this night would certainly be the night in which she would dance on the stars.

The courtyard was quiet, save for the occasional parishioner leaving the chapel after confession—the forgiven on the way home to start anew, never to sin again, or more realistically, to just start again.

One man caught Sister Mary Katherine's attention as he stumbled out of the chapel. The sister watched as another figure stepped from the night's shadows. Now two men walked in the darkened courtyard. As the man stumbled toward the gate, the second man quickened his step.

Under the light of the torch that illuminated the gate, Sister Mary Katherine saw the face of the second man. Drawing a cord from beneath his robe, Father Ignatius absolved the man of his life.

More than a month had passed since that starlit night. Sister Mary Katherine walked through the courtyard in the cool mist of the summer evening. The courtyard was quiet and deserted. The shadows grew larger as she hurried to her room. As she passed the gate, a dark figure stepped from the shadows.

"Sister, I would like to speak with you." Father Ignatius approached Sister Mary Katherine.

"Yes, Father." *Does he know that I saw what he did? Did he see me?* The sister's heart raced.

Father Ignatius took three quick steps. He now stood only inches from Sister Mary Katherine. He is too close. *Stay calm*, she thought. She wanted to run, but she was riveted by fear to the spot where she stood.

"I have something for you." Father Ignatius looked into her frightened eyes. She saw nothing in his eyes—only darkness. Her panic rose. Sister Mary Katherine tried to scream, but no sound came from her throat as Father Ignatius tightened a cord around her neck. *I cannot breathe! I am dying!* Mary Katherine struggled, and then she floated into darkness. *I am dead. This is what it's like. I am dead…*

Sister Mary Katherine awoke. The bed covers were the only foe that she had struggled against. The nightmare plagued her sleeping and also her waking hours.

She wanted to escape the confines of the monastery and return to her father, but the oath that she had sworn to him to stay with the sisters would not allow it. She wanted to tell Theresa Marie about the murder in the courtyard and about her plan. However, fear of the harm that could befall Theresa Marie if she were made privy to Ignatius' deed kept Sister Mary Katherine silent. Her journal was her only confidante.

Tap, tap, tap.

Sister Mary Katherine worked at the typewriter in the archive office as Theresa Marie researched an ancient icon.

"You're getting pretty good on that typewriter." Theresa Marie took two cookies from her deep pocket and passed one to Mary Katherine.

"My speed has improved greatly thanks to you," Mary Katherine.

"What is your name?" Theresa Marie often quizzed Mary Katherine on the invented facts of her life, as they worked in the archives.

"Kristen Herder."

"What is your father's name?"

"Elmer Herder."

"Where were you born?"

"Düsseldorf."

"Quick, tell me your birthday."

"June 19, 1923."

"1921, Mary Katherine, 1921. That makes you nineteen. You keep forgetting."

"1921. I will not forget again."

Tap. Tap. Tap

"Someone is looking for you." Theresa Marie brought Mary Katherine's attention to Sandalphon on the windowsill.

"Oh, he has a note from Stephen. I am worried about him, He has not been himself lately." Mary Katherine took the foil from Sandalphon.

"Maybe he is just having growing pains. Pretty foil," Theresa Marie said as Mary Katherine read the note

"Oh! No. God, Please no!" Mary Katherine ran from the archives, along the halls of the monastery, through the courtyard, past the chapel, and in to the boys' dormitory. Theresa Marie tried to follow, but fell behind before Mary Katherine reached the boys' dormitory. Mary Katherine gasped for air as she ran into the dormitory's parlor and to the dorm mother.

"I must speak to Stephen Hunsberger!"

"Certainly, Sister, you could speak with the boy if he were here, but Stephen has been out all afternoon," the dorm mother said.

"Where is he?"

"I assume he is playing ball with the other boys."

"Where? Where do they play?"

"In the field behind the dormitory."

Sister Mary Katherine ran from the dormitory to the field where the boys were playing. She saw the back of a familiar head as she ran.

"Stephen, thank goodness. Are you all right?" Sister Mary Katherine spun the boy around, only to see he was not Stephen.

"Have you seen Stephen Hunsberger?" she asked.

"No, not since this morning, Sister."

"Where was he?"

"He was going to the attic. He said Father told him he was supposed to clean it for his penance."

Sister Mary Katherine could see Sandalphon perched on the peak of the dormitory's highest gable. Mary Katherine ran back to the dormitory, past the dorm mother and through the parlor and bounded up the stairs, clearing two stairs with each stride. Her heart pounded.

"Stephen! Stephen! Where are you?" Mary Katherine called as she neared the attic door.

"Help me! Please help me!" she cried to the curious boys who had followed her to the attic. Sister Mary Katherine stood on a stool holding Stephen's lifeless body. Her precious friend hung from the rafters.

Sister Theresa Marie found her way to the stairwell and pushed through the boys who had gathered there. The older boys who had helped Sister Mary Katherine bring Stephen down from the rafters stood silently beside her as she cradled Stephen's body.

"Mary Katherine, the priests have come. They have to take Stephen now," Theresa Marie whispered as she knelt beside Mary Katherine who was still holding Stephen.

"No, he cannot have him." Mary Katherine glared at Father Ignatius as he stood with the other priest. Mary Katherine refused to leave her friend. She rocked Stephen in the cradle of her arms and quietly hummed a lullaby.

She whispered, "I will help you, Stephen. I will not let him hurt you again. I promise." Sister Mary Katherine ran her fingers through Stephen's curly blond hair. "He looks like an angel, Theresa." Mary Katherine gently kissed Stephen's forehead and returned to the comfort of her lullaby.

"Mary Katherine, let me help you." Theresa Marie

took Sister Mary Katherine's arm and gently helped her to her feet.

"I would like to go to my room now." Sister Mary Katherine turned from Theresa Marie to Stephen. Sister Theresa Marie gently took her hand and led her from the dormitory.

In the screaming quiet of her room, Sister Mary Katherine took Stephen's note from her pocket. She read the note once again.

Dear Sister,

What I have done is called a mortal sin. It is at that cost that I will be free and Father Ignatius will no longer be able to force the unspeakable acts of his desire upon me. I am unsure of what is to come after this life. Perhaps, however, it is only life that has been my torment and pain and in death there will be a quiet nothing. Pray for me, Sister.

Stephen

145

Sister Mary Katherine opened the journal her father had given her and placed the folded note between the pages.

"Stephen," she whispered.

She laid her head on the journal, tears spilled down her cheeks and onto the blank page of the open journal. Writing appeared under the wet tear stain that had made the page somewhat translucent. The writing was in her father's own hand.

She examined the book and found that each page was an envelope that could be opened by loosening the ties that bound the journal together. Each envelope contained one page that her father had copied from his own journal. The remainder of the night was spent reading her father's thoughts and gaining insight into Kabbalah.

"Mother Gertrude?" Sister Mary Katherine approached the prioress in her office after the morning prayers.

"Yes, child?"

"When I was walking by the river one afternoon, I noticed a deposit of clay." Sister Mary Katherine studied

Mother Gertrude to see if she was listening.

"Yes, go on. Clay by the river?" Mother Mary Gertrude continued studying her notes.

"I would like your permission to bring some of that clay to the basement."

"Why do you want clay in the basement, child?" Mother Gertrude looked up from her reading.

"I want to create a monument, a sculpture, for the monastery in memory of Stephen."

"How much time do you imagine it will take to complete this sculpture?"

"I plan to work steadily for two months, with your permission of course."

"Your own mother was quite an artist. She was truly a talented sculptor. I had the privilege to see some of her work, and if you have inherited any of her talent, I am sure your tribute to Stephen will be beautiful and most appropriate. You may have the clay. I will ask the gardener to bring it to the empty storage room in the basement. You may work in privacy there. If you need anything else, tell him."

"Thank you, Mother Gertrude."

"Two months, Mary Katherine. That is until the end of October. Theresa Marie will not want to do without you for longer than that." Mother Gertrude was trying to be stern, but her eyes betrayed her.

The storage room in the basement was small, but it was large enough for Mary Katherine's purpose. Mother Gertrude had even given her the key to the room so that her work would remain a mystery until the unveiling.

Each day after class, Sister Mary Katherine worked in the privacy of her basement studio until vespers. Then after supper, she began again. She was often in the basement until the time came for Morning Prayer. When she grew tired and could no longer work, she would study her father's journal. Day after day, week after week, Mary Katherine worked. Finally, she finished, and the next day would be the long-awaited unveiling. Sister Mary Katherine would spend one more night with her creation.

Tap, tap, tap.

"Mary Katherine, it is beginning to storm," Theresa Marie said through the door. "Are you going to come out? I have made tea for us, and I have four nice cookies, one for each of our hands, just as we like. Will you have tea with me finally, Mary Katherine?"

"I will, Theresa Marie, but not now," Mary Katherine called. "I will be all right. I will see you in only a little while, and we will have tea and cookies before bed. I promise. I will be finished soon." Mary Katherine politely dismissed her friend.

"You should be in your room during such a storm, not in this damp basement, Mary Katherine!" Theresa Marie insisted. She would not be easily dismissed.

"I will be up soon. I promise."

"You are a stubborn child, Mary Katherine." Theresa Marie left the basement for the safety of her room.

"Yes." A thunderous boom and a lightning flash filled the basement as Sister Mary Katherine admired her work.

"There you are, Eliakim."

The morning sun rose on the day of the long awaited unveiling. The sisters were gathered in the courtyard, anxious to see what Mary Katherine had created.

"And it shall come to pass that I will call my servant Eliakim...and the key to the house of David, I will lay on his shoulder; so he shall open and none shall shut, and he shall shut, and none shall open." Mother Mary Gertrude read from the book of Isaiah.

After the dedication ceremony, the sisters all commented on the beauty and realistic features and of his handsome face. Mary Katherine's Eliakim was a wondrous creation. The sisters crowded around Mary Katherine.

"He looks so real, Mary Katherine."

"Every muscle and every feature is so defined."

Eliakim stood more than two meters tall. Muscles bulged beneath his robe and cloak. Eliakim's face was the image of a handsome man looking to the heavens. One of his muscular arms was raised to the heavens while the other held a key in his clenched fist at his shoulder. He was magnificent to be certain.

CHAPTER NINE

CONFESSION

"Duetzman!" The SS officer leaned over Ignatius's desk. "Perhaps you have forgotten why you were posted here." The officer leaned closer and snarled into his subordinate's face, "It is not so you can enjoy the company of young boys. I know the sisters are hiding children of the Jews here. You, Duetzman, are here to seek out the offspring of the vermin who has infested our country and report to me. I know the sisters are hiding children here." The officer spat his words. "Be well advised, Duetzman, you will find yourself serving the Fuehrer in the ranks if I find that you are not diligent in your search!" The officer turned on his mark and left Ignatius in his study.

"Father?" Sister Mary Katherine stood at the threshold of the open door.

"Yes, Sister Mary Katherine?"

"Mother Gertrude asks if you will you join us for dinner after mass next week on All Saints' Day?"

"Yes, I will be joining you. Thank you for the invitation."

Sister Mary Katherine silently left his office

Ignatius wondered how long she had been standing there before she made herself known. These women skulk up and down the halls of this place like ghosts... A person never knows where they are lurking. The niece of the prioress could cause trouble for him. Ignatius was determined to guard his purpose.

Preparations for the All Saints' Day feast began early. Every sister who was available had a responsibility, and they worked diligently to complete their tasks before the evening mass.

"*Potatoes*! I need potatoes. Nobody brought the potatoes up from the cellar!" Sister Mary Francis called out to whoever was in hearing distance. Sister Mary Francis was the undisputed queen of the kitchen. In truth, she was the saint of the kitchen.

"I will get the potatoes and maybe a rutabaga or two if we have any," Mother Gertrude said.

Escaping for a few moments to the root cellar was Mother Gertrude's guilty pleasure. The cool air and the earth's musky perfume rose from the root cellar and lightened Mother Gertrude's head. Mother Gertrude made her way up the steep wooden stairs with her apron full of potatoes and a few nice rutabagas. She could see a dark shadow of a man standing at the cellar door.

"Mother Gertrude, may I have a moment of your time?" Father Ignatius stood at the top of the steps. Mother Gertrude's exit was blocked.

"Father, may I pass please? They are expecting me in the kitchen with these vegetables."

"I asked for a moment of your time, Mother."

Mother Gertrude tensed. "I really need to get these

vegetables to the kitchen," she said, moving up a step.

Father Ignatius took Mother Gertrude by her shoulder and pulled her to himself. The vegetables spilled from Mother Gertrude's apron and bounced down the steps.

"Father, what do you want of me?"

"I want to know what you know." Father Ignatius gripped Mother Gertrude even tighter.

"I do not understand, Father." Mother Gertrude winced as Father Ignatius dug his fingers into her shoulder.

"You worthless old woman, I want the truth. Tell me what you know now! What has Sister Mary Katherine told you?" Father Ignatius was determined. He stepped alongside Mother Gertrude.

"The only truth that I know comes from our Lord's holy word, Ignatius. Do not be deceived. God is not mocked, for whatever a man sows, that he shall also reap." Mother Gertrude spoke the words only seconds before one forceful push sent her tumbling down the stairs.

"You disgust me, Mother!" Father Ignatius called down the dark staircase. He spoke as much to his own mother as to Mother Gertrude.

Father Ignatius opened the cellar doors and walked into the fading light of the late afternoon. As Mother Gertrude's broken body lie on the cold stone floor of the root cellar, Ignatius returned to his study to prepare his sermon for the evening mass.

Sister Mary Katherine finished setting the dining tables just as Sister Mary Francis began shouting for potatoes once again.

"If I do not start the potatoes soon, there will be none! Will someone see what Mother Gertrude is doing?" Sister Mary Francis said as she put pies into the hot oven.

"I will go to help, Mother," Sister Mary Katherine said.

The afternoons were cooling quickly, and the days were growing shorter. Mary Katherine pulled her cloak close and hurried to the root cellar. It has been more than a year since she came to live at the monastery. During that time Mary Katherine had learned the beliefs of the sisters. She had lived by her understanding and the oath that she had sworn to her father, and now she had a great respect for the sisters and their commitment to their beliefs. The sisters dedication to one another and Mother Gertrude's unwavering gentle kindness had made her realize how much she had grown to love them.

"Mother? Are you down there? Mary Francis is still calling for potatoes." Mary Katherine started down the steps. A low moan rose from the dark cellar.

"Mother Gertrude?" Another moan, almost inaudible, ascended the staircase. Mary Katherine hurried down the dark stairwell, alarmed by the sound of the quiet moaning.

"Mother Gertrude, where are you? Are you alright?" Mary Katherine stumbled in the darkness that was relieved only slightly by the waning afternoon light that struggled through the cracks in the cellar door. Her hands searched the dark wall for the lantern

"Matches, matches. Light the lantern. The lantern, light the lantern." Mary Katherine's words directed her frantic hands.

She broke two matches before she succeeded in lighting the lantern.

"Mother!" Mary Katherine knelt beside the mother

superior and placed her ear on the old woman's chest.

"Breathing, she's breathing. I must get help. The other sisters will help me take you upstairs, Mother. I need help." Mary Katherine rose to her feet. Mother Gertrude grasped the hem of Mary Katherine's habit. "Mother, let me go. I must bring help."

"Ignatius…" Mother Gertrude whispered her last word.

"This is the last time we will come to the grotto for a while, Sandalphon. It is becoming much too cold. The trees are bare, and everything has gone to gray. Are you cold, Sandalphon?" It was not as much the cold as it was the overwhelming sense of loss that would keep Sister Mary Katherine from her quiet respites in the grotto. Her thoughts were of the afternoon in the root cellar and Mother Gertrude's last words. She was certain that Mother Gertrude had not whispered Father Ignatius's name in her final moment because she wanted his final absolution.

"Sandalphon, I must make confession tonight."

The shadow of the large black bird that circled above

the sister as she walked back to the monastery lent a somber shade of contrast to the winter day.

Sister Mary Katherine closed the door to the confessional.

"Father?"

"Yes, child?" Ignatius was confused. She did not begin her confession with the words "Forgive me, Father."

"Do you believe the Holy Scripture is true?"

"Are you questioning your faith, Sister?" Father Ignatius recognized Mary Katherine's voice.

"No, Father. I am not."

"Then what is your confession, Sister?"

"Father, do you believe the priests and prophets are held to a higher standard, just as the Holy Scripture states?"

"If the scriptures are true, then certainly it is of no consequence what I believe."

"That is true, Father. So consequence must be in relationship to one's action."

"I suppose that is true, Sister."

"According to the Holy Scriptures, Father, if a man

158

causes harm to come to one of God's own, his fate would be better if he were tossed into the sea with a millstone bound around his neck."

"Is there a point to your cryptic questions, Mary Katherine?" Ignatius snarled.

"Yes, Ignatius. Stephen and Mother Gertrude will be your millstone. I bid you good night." Sister Mary Katherine quietly left the confessional.

That night, Sister Mary Katherine's words and dreams of young boys who cried out to be returned to their innocence haunted Ignatius's bed.

November 8, 1940

The SS officer appeared at the door to Father Ignatius's study. "Your report, Duetzman."

"Good morning, sir. I did not expect you to be back so soon."

"I want your report, Duetzman, not whining excuses." The officer sat on the edge of Ignatius's desk and lit a cigarette as Ignatius leafed through papers. The opportunity to rid himself of the odd Mary Katherine sat before him.

"I don't believe the sisters are hiding any of the Jewish children. None of the children here seem out of place. Although…" He paused, "there is one young sister I have concerns about."

"Her name, Duetzman?" The officer demanded.

"Her name is Mary Katherine. She came here not long ago."

"Take me to her."

The sound of the small troop echoed, through the monastery halls, and across the courtyard as they marched. Father Ignatius led the troop to the convent school and finally into Sister Mary Katherine's classroom.

"Sister Mary Katherine, I would like to speak with you," Father Ignatius said.

"Children, continue to quietly work on your English conversation." Sister Mary Katherine turned from the chalkboard, dropped the chalk into her pocket, and addressed Father Ignatius.

"How may I help you, Father?" Sister Mary Katherine's eyes found the soldiers at her classroom door.

"The officer has come to question some of us. I am

sure there is nothing to worry about." Father Ignatius's words were for the benefit of the sisters who had followed the troop to Mary Katherine's classroom.

"What is your name?" The officer was a formidable presence. He towered over the frightened Mary Katherine.

"Sister Mary Katherine." She trembled as she drew her strength to speak.

"What is your birth name?"

"Kristen Herder."

"No middle name?"

"Emma. It is Emma."

"Father's name?" The officer recorded each answer into his note pad.

"Elmer Daniel Herder."

"Mother's name?"

"Hilda Ingra Herder."

"Where were you born?"

"Düsseldorf."

"How old are you?"

"Nineteen."

"When is your birth date?"

"June 19, 1923." Sister Mary Katherine's eyes found her friend. Theresa Marie's breath caught in her throat. Mary Katherine had answered with her actual birthday. The officer continued his questioning, seemingly unaware of the age discrepancy.

"Your mother's maiden name?"

Sister Mary Katherine opened her mouth, but her mind would not give up a name.

"Your mother's maiden name, Sister." The officer stepped toward Sister Mary Katherine as he repeated the question "What is your mother's maiden name? That is not so hard a question, Sister."

"Schliemann, Schliemann. Her maiden name was Schliemann."

"Schliemann? You seem uncertain, Sister. Was your mother's name Schliemann or was it not, Sister?" The officer circled Sister Mary Katherine like a hyena as he fired the barrage of questions.

"Yes, it was Schliemann." Sister Mary Katherine's eyes rimmed with tears.

"You are crying. Is something wrong?"

"My parents were killed in a house fire only recently. I am still sad when I think of them."

"Where is your faith, Sister? Were they not good people? Surely, you trust that they are in heaven with your God. I would like to see your room now."

"My room?"

"Yes, your room. I see no problem with that, do you, Sister?"

"No, sir, no problem."

Sister Mary Katherine led the troop back into the monastery, through the priory halls, and to her room. Sister Mary Katherine's cot was neatly made. A large crucifix, the room's only adornment, stood on the bureau. Her writing table was clear.

"Search the bureau and the bed," the officer ordered his troop.

The soldiers ripped Sister Mary Katherine's mattress apart and searched her bureau drawers. The officer opened the drawer of her writing table.

"What is this?" The officer held the gold ring—that Sandalphon had brought her at their first meeting in the grotto.

"I found it on the ground," Mary Katherine said.

"This ring has a Hebrew inscription. It must have belonged to a Jew. Why would you keep this piece of trash?"

Sister Mary Katherine remained silent. She could not say the initials engraved inside the band identified the ring as belonging to her mother, Sara Rosa Davidson.

"I am waiting for an answer, good Sister." The officer said, sneering.

"I thought it was pretty," she whispered.

"No. I think there is another reason you kept it, and be assured I will find that reason."

The officer joined the three soldiers who now stood at the door to Mary Katherine's room. He spoke quietly to his troops and then turned to Sister Mary Katherine.

"Is it so that you teach English, Sister?"

"Yes."

"It is fortunate for the children you do not teach mathematics, Sister, as a simple calculation would put your age as eighteen, not nineteen. Take her!" The officer barked the order to his troop. Sister Mary Katherine was led through the halls by the officer. She was flanked on both sides by a soldier, the fourth soldier closed ranks behind.

"Where are you taking me?" Sister Mary Katherine asked. The officer pushed her into the back of a transport vehicle.

CHAPTER TEN

BOOG

The stench of urine, feces, vomit, and musty clothing emanated from the detainment center. The interrogation room held one chair that was positioned directly beneath a solitary light strung by a single cord from the low ceiling. The room smelled of fear. Sister Mary Katherine smelled of fear.

Early morning grew into afternoon, and Sister Mary Katherine still sat alone in the interview room. There were rumors she had heard, rumors of towns where the entire Jewish population had been detained. Some of the rumors told of camps where the Jews had been taken and of the unspeakable horrors that had awaited them there. However, there was no proof of the truth to these rumors—no proof at all since no one who had been taken had ever come back to attest to the atrocities. No one had ever come back.

The SS officer burst through the door in a matter of two long strides he stood towering over Sister Mary Katherine. "What's your name?"

"Sister Mary Kather–" A loud crack rang out as her head hit the back of the chair with the force of the officer's blow. The stinging of her cheek and the taste of blood in her mouth was the officer's statement of intent to Miriam.

"I want your birth name."

"Kristen Emma Herder." Another hard slap. Sister Mary Katherine's cheek burned with the impression of the man's hand. Tears fell from Sister Mary Katherine's eyes, but she did not cry out. A closed fist blow fell to her opposite cheek.

"Do you see the papers in my hand? They tell me that Kristen Herder, the daughter of Hilda and Elmer Herder, never existed in Düsseldorf or anywhere else, as of that matter."

"Miriam Ruth Davidson. My name is Miriam." As the *result* of a sustaining strength, Miriam fearlessly looked into the face of the officer.

"A Jew."

"Yes, I am." Miriam did not break her gaze.

"One of the chosen?" the officer sneered. "Well, chosen one, take the habit off. We can't have you sitting around looking like a Catholic, now can we?"

Miriam removed her habit. She stood in the mound of black wool and white linen, facing the leering officer wearing only her black cotton slip and leggings.

"Turn around," he ordered.

Miriam turned her back to the officer. The air split with the sharp sound of a rod repeatedly hitting her tiny back. Miriam fell to her knees but she still did not cry out. The officer pulled Miriam to her feet and threw her across the room.

"Tie her to the chair."

Two soldiers crowded into the small room. The soldiers tossed Miriam into the hard chair. They bound Miriam's feet to the chair's legs while the officer bound her hands to the chair's arms.

"Where are you from?"

"Tuttinger," Miriam whispered.

"Tuttinger? What is your father's name, child?" The

168

officer's tone suddenly changed.

"Jacob Nathaniel Davidson."

"Jacob Davidson. We have been looking for him and his comrades for more than a year."

The officer squatted in front of Miriam. His enormous hands encompassed her head. He pulled her face within an inch of his own. "Where are your father and his friends? Tell me where they are now, and it will be easier for you later." The officer lit a cigarette and waited for an answer.

"I do not know where they are. I swear. I do not know." The officer smothered his cigarette on Miriam's bare shoulder and left the room.

Miriam could not determine the number of hours she had been tied to the chair. The sting of the officer's fist had left her cheek, replaced by a dull throb. The welts across her back wept, and her shoulder burned. She did not cry, but her bladder screamed. The dread of humiliation could not control her bodily functions much longer.

"We begin again, Jew." The officer leaned over Miriam. She did not acknowledge the officer. He wound his fingers around a handful of her hair and yanked her head back until they were face to face. Miriam winced. The officer dropped a handful of hair to the floor.

"That is better." I like to see your pretty face. Your... pretty...Jew...face." The officer traced Miriam's features with his finger, spat in her face, and then wiped the spittle from Miriam's cheek to her lips.

"Where are your father and his friends?"

Miriam spat. The officer simply knelt in front of Miriam, balancing on one knee.

"Take your time, think about it. I have time, you see. I can come and go as I like. I can eat and drink. I can do what I care to. I am not tied to a chair. So please, think about your answer. Take your time." He stared into Miriam's eyes. Miriam stared into the abysmal darkness that was the officer's soul.

"You filthy bitch!" The officer jumped to his feet. His boot, the cuff of his pants, and his knee were wet with urine. The chair Miriam was bound to hit the floor as a result of the force of the officer's blow to her head.

The officer left the room again; the soldiers righted

170

Miriam in the overturned chair. Miriam sat motionless in the chair until the officer and the two soldiers returned sometime later with a fourth man. The man stood in the in the corner of the room. He held a small wooden box in his hands; his eyes searched the room. The man mumbled incoherently as he shifted his enormous weight from foot to foot, the wooden box tightly pressed against his protruding stomach. Even though the setting of the sun had cooled the room considerably, the man's bald head shone with beads of greasy sweat. His once-white undershirt was wet with perspiration, and a ring of black filth encircled the neckline and dipped down to a point in the middle of the man's chest, drawing Miriam's eye to the man's dandling, ruptured navel. A bombastic sound escaped the man's buttocks, followed by a noxious odor. Miriam glanced toward the man.

"Pay no attention to Boog. He's just waiting." The officer smiled.

"Yes, sir." Miriam's head swam. She did not recognize her own voice. Miriam floated above herself. *This is not happening to me. This is happening to someone else. He cannot hurt me. He cannot hurt me.*

"Your father, I want to know where your father is. Can he create a golem?"

"I swear, I do not know," Miriam mumbled. Her own voice was foreign to her.

"Can you create a golem?"

"I don't know what you mean."

The enraged officer lifted the chair that Miriam was bound to and flung it across the room. The chair and Miriam miraculously landed in an upright position.

The officer sighed. "I have lost my temper again. I am sorry. I never know where it will take me. I think you are a very pretty little Jew. If you cooperate and begin to answer my questions, I will consider keeping you for myself. I have always wanted a Jew of my own." The officer lifted Miriam's face with the end of the rod that he had beaten her with and studied her. "You would make a delicious little pet." He lit another cigarette. "How rude of me. May I offer you a cigarette?" The officer flicked a burning ember onto Miriam's shoulder. "How many men left with your father?" Another ember fell to Miriam's shoulder.

"I do not know." Another ember burned deep into

Miriam's soft flesh. Miriam closed her eyes. "It is not me," she whispered.

She peered down at herself from the ceiling as the officer doused the remainder of his cigarette on the side of her neck.

"We are not finished with you yet, but now, it's Boog's turn."

Boog moved toward Miriam, still tightly clutching the wooden box to his substantial belly. Muttering to himself, he searched the light cord hanging above Miriam's head and found an electrical outlet. The apparatus he took from the box made a high-pitched squeal when plugged into the outlet. Boog manipulated the instrument, which alternated between a high-pitched squeal and a steady hum. One of the soldiers pushed a stool under Boog's ample hindquarters as he sat.

Miriam watched the top of Boog's bald head. Pores expelled tiny rivers of greasy, glistening sweat that dripped down his forehead and into his heavy brow. Boog touched Miriam's hand she gasped in fear.

A drop of sweat reached the corner of Boog's eye. He cocked his head upward to brush the salty drop away.

As Miriam looked into Boog's soft blue eyes, crystal white flashes of light shone from Boog's soul.

"I am sorry," Boog's sad, full lips mouthed as the officer handed him a piece of paper. Boog gently untied Miriam's hand and retied it palm side up. She quietly allowed him to tattoo the inside of her forearm. Boog's eyes darted between his work on the tattoo and the officer while he spoke quietly to the soldiers.

"What about him?" one of the soldiers asked.

"Boog? He is deaf and addle-brained. Ignore him," the officer continued instructing the soldiers.

Upon completion of his work, Boog returned his tools and the scrap of paper to the box. He received a few cents from the officer and, still muttering, left the room. Boog shuffled through the streets and alleys, moving closer to the sound of laughter and music, but he heard nothing on his way to the Rathskeller.

Three men of the Miter Stand, the brave German freedom fighters, sat at a table in the corner of the crowded tavern. One of the men motioned to Boog.

"What did you see?" the man turned toward Boog as

174

he spoke.

"Young girl, a nun. They have been rough with her." Boog wrote these words on a notepad he took from his jacket. Boog watched the man's lips as he spoke.

"How many soldiers? Could you see what they said? Where are they taking her?"

"Au, but first detainment center for questioning. They look for her father and the Kabbalah. They move her tonight, soon. Two soldiers and captain." Boog scribbled the words on his notepaper.

The leader of the group spoke to the band of men, "Au, Auschwitz. Detainment center. Her father must a Kabbalist. They will not take her to the camp yet. They want more information. She will go to the other center tonight. We can intercept them at the crossroads just beyond the forest. There will be only two or three of them. We will take the girl easily,"

Miriam no longer ached from restraints that held her much tighter than necessary. She had lost all feeling in her hands. She could not recognize her own fingers, once alabaster they were now the blue grey shade of sculpting clay.

The officer returned to the chair where Miriam was bound. He placed his enormous foot in the center of her chest and with a swift push sent her forcefully crashing to the floor. White light exploded in Miriam's eyes as her head hit the floor. The officer untied Miriam's hands, leaving her feet bound.

"You have one more guest. He has been waiting patiently to speak with you." The officer nodded to the soldier, who opened the door and allowed the "guest" to enter.

Ignatius stood over Miriam. The uniform that he wore identified him as an SS officer. Ignatius heavy boot found Miriam's ribs several times as she lay on the floor. Still tied to the overturned chair, she struggled to no avail to right herself in the chair. Ignatius laughed, righted the chair, and crouched in front of her. Miriam gasped for air.

"Father Ignatius," Miriam moaned.

"I have been curious about one thing for some time now. I wonder how you knew of Stephen's death so quickly. How were you alerted?"

"A note. Stephen sent me a note telling me everything." Miriam looked into Ignatius's eyes. Ignatius turned away.

"And did you keep this note?" Ignatius paced, he did not know the exact contents of the note that this woman held, but he feared that if in actuality the boy had sent an explicit note he certainly would no longer be able to hide himself in the church.

"Yes, I did." Miriam held her gaze on Ignatius. She would not blink. She had won this game many times in the schoolyard.

"Tell me where the note is," Ignatius demanded.

Miriam's gaze remained fixed, but she was silent.

"Tell me where the note is. Tell me!" Enraged, Ignatius's hands flew to Miriam's tiny neck. The chair fell back to the floor. Ignatius fell on top of Miriam and continued to squeeze. "I will kill you. I will kill you and find the note."

"Ignatius, stop!" the officer in charge demanded. "She has to go to the detainment center for further questioning. You will not have the pleasure of ending her." The officer pulled Ignatius to his feet, breaking the chokehold he had on

Miriam's neck. Ignatius leaned close to Miriam.

"I will find that note. I will certainly find that note," Ignatius hissed.

"No, Ignatius, you will never."

"Enough, Jew. Untie your feet and get dressed."

The officer turned to the soldiers. "We will process her here, and then we will deliver her to the center. They will transport her to the camp when they finish questioning her."

"But, sir, you said we could have her first," one of the soldiers reminded the captain.

"Not here…somewhere on the road. If we leave now, you will be back to your post before dawn." The soldiers marched their prisoner down the narrow hall.

November 9, 1940

Against the light of the full moon, Miriam could see Sandalphon perched on top of the transport vehicle. A sharp thrust from one of the soldiers sent Miriam wheeling into the back of the truck.

As the soldiers were closing the door, the raven

swooped through the darkness and into the back of the vehicle.

"What was that?" The younger soldier stepped back from the vehicle.

"It looked like a bat," The second soldier said, he nudged the younger soldier toward the back of the vehicle. "You should flush it out." The soldier nudged the younger soldier again.

"No, I will not. The bat will bite me. Let the bat have her for all I care."

"He's right. She's not worth getting rabies. Come, forget her. We will get a whore in Düsseldorf," the captain assured his men of their reward.

The observation light dimly lit the back of the vehicle. Miriam found Sandalphon in the shadows and pulled herself closer to him. She used the last bit of her strength to reach him. She held him close, breathing in his comfort.

"I am hurt, Sandalphon. I need help. I cannot go where they are taking me." Miriam coughed, blood poured from her mouth. She wiped the blood from her mouth onto her sleeve and, gathering her strength, she pulled herself up and leaned against the bench attached to the wall of the vehicle, she perched Sandalphon on her lap. Her eyes rolled like marbles inside her clouded head. Her world spun in slow motion.

Miriam closed her eyes, when she opened them Sandalphon was still perched on her lap. She did not know if a minute or an hour had passed.

"Did I sleep, Sandalphon? Time... My father, spirit realm, time is not kept. The spirit realm...time. Jacob's ladder, father, the door, ladders, many doors..." Miriam closed her eyes again. A moment later, she reopened them.

"I dreamed, Sandalphon. I dreamed I spoke with father. Then I climbed Jacob's ladder. I could see time traveling in all directions. I saw time spiraling around and jutting out and then connecting to another spiral—repeatedly spiraling, jutting out, and then connecting. There was no backward or forward, no up or down or sideways. I then saw a being. He shone like the sun. I thought, '*If this is God and I look into his face, I will surely die.*' I looked into his face, but I saw no features. Instead, I saw everything. I saw all existence, everything. Everyone who has been or ever will be on Earth made up his countenance. He did not speak words, but he told me he would take me somewhere. He reached out to me, and I to him. We touched. Then, I awoke."

Miriam's crucifix glinted in the dim light. Miriam lifted it from the floor where it had fallen and returned it to her deep pocket. A piece of broken blackboard chalk touched her finger. Miriam retrieved the crucifix and the chalk.

"Jacob's ladder," Miriam whispered she slid to the black floor of the vehicle and began to draw.

"Circles, circles, circles. Lines connect circles... lines, lines, lines." A supernatural strength sustained Miriam as she began to scribble on the floor of the vehicle. The night air grew heavy with the impending storm. Thunder rolled, in the distance, lightning lit the night sky. Each flash of light drew closer to the vehicle.

"Where did this storm come from?" The young soldier asked. He struggled to see the road through the torrential rain.

"It was not on the horizon when we left. Perhaps it will pass. Look in the back see what the girl is doing," The captain closed his eyes to sleep while the storm raged.

"She is on the floor. Maybe she's dead."

"Jacob's ladder. Now, I will go into the spirit realm, Sandalphon," Miriam whispered as she took in Sandalphon's essence in one last comforting breath. Miriam had scribbled the rungs of Jacobs's ladder across the floor of the vehicle. She sharpened the end of the silver crucifix on the gritty floor. With one deliberate move, she cut deeply from the bottom of her palm, across her entire wrist. Upon Jacob's ladder, scrawled in chalk on the floor of a prisoners transport vehicle, Miriam's life passed, and Sandalphon returned to clay.

At the precise moment of Miriam's escape into the spirit realm, lightning split the sky above the vehicle. The brilliant flash contrasted the dark night, momentary blinding the driver and sending the vehicle down the embankment.

"Are you all right?" The young soldier shook his head, trying to regain his vision.

"Yes, I am. But we better check the girl." the older soldier said.

Four men of the Miter Stand crouched at the edge of the forest, hiding in the deep thicket. The men watched as the soldiers climbed out of the disabled vehicle.

"Shit, the door has flown open," the older soldier cursed.

"What the hell happened here?" The officer bellowed.

"A lightning strike, a direct hit, sir." The soldiers peered into the back of the truck.

"She must have escaped when the door flew open. This will not go well for us if we do not find her. She could not have gotten far. Come hurry, we must find her," the captain said.

"Look!" The young soldier pointed to the roof inside the vehicle.

"How can that be? What would cause the roof to explode out?"

Neither soldier had an explanation for the officer.

The men of the Miter Stand watched the soldiers begin their search. They whispered among themselves.

"She was not in the truck."

"She has escaped."

"We will return with more men. We know the forest. We will find her."

"What about the SS?" one of the men asked.

"We have a marksman. He will take them easily."
With three quick shots from his rifle, Boog ended the
soldier's search.

"We will push the truck and the bodies down into
the ravine. It will go unnoticed there. At daybreak, we will
without a doubt find the girl."

CHAPTER ELEVEN

THE PHILOSOPHER'S STONE

"Cold mutton, bread, and cheese—a very fine breakfast indeed. My stomach could not be any more satisfied if I were king." Alden pushed back from the table, jiggled his sizeable belly, and laughed. The entire table toasted the spectacle with a cup of goat milk.

"Today, Jacob, Auvil, and I will begin on the Philosopher's Stone." Alden took a very large emerald brooch from his trouser pocket and laid it on the table for the men to see. "This is a donation from our host, Lord Smithe." The men gasped at the size of the jewel. "We all know the traditional accounts of the philosopher's stone, and the emerald tablet. It is told that the secret of the elixir was written on an emerald tablet. The secrets of the emerald tablet have been handed down to us from generation to generation. However the tablet has never been found. I believe the tablet is a myth, but an emerald *is* the key. An emerald must be distilled to its pure essence, and that will become the Philosopher's Stone. I am certain of that, and I am certain that using Auvil to carry out the process will finally enable us to extract the pure essence from the emerald. I understand that some of you are reluctant to delegate this responsibility to the golems, but this distillation must be carried out with no greed or avarice."

"Auvil will perform the process without such qualities. Thus the principals that have been taught to us will finally allow us to extract the pure essence from the emerald. While Jacob, Auvil and I begin with this process, the rest of you will work together. You will create two more golems like Auvil. You will grow the essence that we use to create the Homunculi. That will take forty days as you know. However, after the forty days the essence will be built into the Kabbalists' golems. If we are successful in our endeavors we will have all the specialized lab assistance we need.

The men then left the laboratory to begin their

combined task.

"I have learned much from you, Jacob," Alden said.

"And I from you," Jacob acknowledged. "Before our acquaintance, I thought that Alchemists were interested only in the quest to change lead to gold."

Alden smiled. "Regrettably, that's the thought most have about Alchemists. They imagine maniacs adding concoctions to lead to form gold or dripping solutions on rocks and pebbles to change them to diamonds and rubies. The truth is that the Alchemist works to better the plight of mankind, but the human avarice has always interfered with attaining that goal. However, now we have Auvil, who has no avarice for precious metals or gemstones, giving us the great success we will soon see and will continue to see. Jacob, my friend, Auvil is more valuable than all the gold in England; unfortunately the madman across the channel is also aware of his value."

"Where shall we begin, Alden?"

"We will ready the retort for the distillation, and then we will have Auvil begin the process."

Many hours passed with Auvil working as he was instructed. Beakers were filled and emptied and filled over again. The retort hissed as steam traveled through twisted tubes, the highway that would eventually lead to the success that the Alchemists and their predecessors have sought for centuries. Finally, the retort yielded the precious elixir. Jacob and Alden examined the liquid in the tiny bottle, but they did not remove the bottle from the clutches of the retort.

"What shall we do with it?" Jacob asked.

"Nothing," Alden replied. "It's still in Auvil's purpose."

Alden directed Auvil to retrieve the tiny bottle from the retort. Jacob and Alden stood riveted to the sight as their creation obeyed. With utmost attention, Auvil turned the retort's latch. He carefully retrieved the precious elixir, the elixir that they believe will be the most powerful solution known to man: The Philosopher's Stone!

Immediately as Auvil bore the majik into the world, Jacob and Alden were in the midst of a force not completely unlike an electrical storm. Jacob and Alden stood surrounded by a fantastic crackling, swirling light show of static electricity. The men turned in all directions. They were engulfed in the energy. Finally, Alden turned to Jacob and unexpectedly burst into laughter.

"Jacob!" Alden laughed. "You should see yourself. The hair on your head is standing straight up."

"And if you had any hair on the top of your head, it would be on its ends also." Jacob laughed and continued, "As it is, only that bit of fuzz around your face is standing out like a lion's mane. What do you suppose this phenomenon is?"

"I am not completely certain, but it seems to be a wall or a cocoon of energy," Alden said, running a hand down his face.

"Now we must harness it," Jacob remarked as Alden studied the arcs of static that were displaying around him. "Auvil, now place the stopper lying next to the retort into the neck of the bottle," Jacob said.

Auvil again obeyed precisely, and the maelstrom of static electricity dissipated immediately.

"We must go now to gather our men," Alden said. "This is splendid! There will be a great deal of discussion before we continue."

"Yes, Alden, in the council of many, there is great wisdom."

Jacob, Alden, and Auvil left the laboratory and sought out the others. As the men sat in their quarters deep in discussion of the events of the day, the vendor's daughter, Lydia, walked from her home. Her rickety pull cart clacked on each roll of its wooden wheels. As Lydia neared the edge of the village, a familiar woman stepped beside her.

"Where are you going so late in the evening with your wagon so laden? What do you have there?" the woman said.

"Oh, good evening, Mistress Clarisse," Lydia greeted. "Well, I say evening, but I think it's really only late afternoon. Either way, it's lovely. How are you today?" Lydia smiled hoping that the woman would think her addled and question her no more.

"I say you have grown into a fine young woman Lydia. That seems quite a heavy wagon. Where are you headed?" Mistress Clarisse insisted.

"I'm going to the Vicar with a pot of mutton stew and these clothes for the poor box."

"That's quite a large pot of stew for one lonely Vicar."

Lydia twirled one long, dark curl around her finger as she spoke, "My mum thinks the Vicar has a guest."

"I see. Well, you better get on your way." Mistress Clarisse turned and walked back to her home. She unlocked the three locks that secured her privacy and opened the door. In the quiet seclusion of her dimly lit room, she pulled a suitcase from beneath her bed and fashioned the odd parts that lie inside into a radio transmitter.

"Lydia is traveling to the outskirts of the village," she reported.

"Watch her closely."

Lydia continued to the barn her destination and her mission.

The long walk to the cobbler gave Jacob and Alden the chance to revisit the discussion of the night before. Auvil followed Jacob and Alden as they left the cobbler and walked toward the edge of the village.

"I think that Seth was right about the lodestone." Jacob thought out loud.

"Yes, he is absolutely correct," Alden said. The

natural magnetism of lodestone is exactly what we need. When we get back, we will start distilling it. Imagine how powerful it will be in its pure essence. How does that boot feel, Jacob?"

Jacob smiled. "It feels as good as new. I cannot even imagine the power we might unleash, but we will soon see."

"AUVIL, FIRE! JACOB, TURN AROUND!" Again, Jacob heard Aaron's voice from within the village. Jacob turned around; Auvil had also turned around and now stood motionless. A woman walked a few meters behind them. Upon Jacob turning the woman hastily crossed to the opposite side of the pebble strewn road, and scurried into the alley.

"Who was that woman?" Jacob said.

"Mistress Clarisse. She teaches the children," Alden explained. "I don't know her well, even though she grew up here. She's either very shy or just standoffish. I could never decide. Her family was well respected for the fact that her father was a war hero from The Great War."

"The Great War…" Jacob looked wistfully at the sky. "I have heard it called that. Also it has been called The War to End All Wars. I fear what is coming will dwarf the dreadfulness of that war. Do you think she knows you're an Alchemist Alden?"

"Only a handful of trusted friends and family know, and they would never betray our trust."

"Do you think she's a Nazi sympathizer?" Jacob asked.

"There has been speculation," Alden said. "Only because her mother was a German war bride her father brought home with him, but her mother was a good woman."

"I ask because I heard Aaron warning me again. We must beware."

"My fear, Jacob, is that you are correct."

More than three month's time had passed since Auvil extracted the essence of the Philosopher's Stone. Jacob and Alden have worked tirelessly directing Auvil in the continuing process, and their men in the labor of obtaining enough lodestone to extract a sufficient amount of its pure essence.

"This has been slow going, I must say," Alden spoke.

"Yes, it has," Jacob said, not wavering from his task

of sorting out the magnetic rocks from the large pile the men had collected.

"I believe now we have enough lodestone, Jacob. Or should I say I believe I have lifted enough lodestone for a lifetime."

"Jacob, Alden. May I speak with you?" Bertram, the eldest and most respected of Alden's company, asked.

"What is it, Bertram? Have you a quandary?" Alden said.

"No, I require your opinion. Please come." Bertram turned quickly and left the laboratory.

Jacob and Alden exchanged a quizzical glance and suspended their endeavors. They followed Bertram to the barn. In the barn, all of the men stood naked in a semicircle facing Alden and Jacob as they entered. Alden was the first to comment.

"Yes, Bertram, they are defiantly naked. Is that all?" Alden stated without wit or smirk.

"Ah, but look, Alden, our men have invited guests to their festivity." Jacob added.

"Why, yes, they have. Bertram, introduce these

194

newcomers." Alden laughed he could no longer hold back his amusement with the men's frivolity. Bertram, Alden, and Jacob crossed the barn and stood in front of the two naked golems.

"This is Belenus," Bertram introduced, the first of the two. Belenus was the smaller of the golems. However, his fierce countenance shrouded his smaller size. "Belenus is the ruler of fire. It is a strong Celtic name, well befitting a golem. Do you agree, Alden?"

Alden laughed heartily. "That's a fine name. And the next, what do you propose to call him?"

"This is Gideon," Bertram said. "Do you accept that name, Jacob?" Gideon was quite large. He even topped Auvil by a few centimeters.

"Gideon is a superb name. His own mother could not have named him more appropriately. They are both magnificent and will serve us well." Jacob patted Bertram's back. The men cheered as they pulled their pants back on.

"Tonight, make merry. Tomorrow, we put them to work," Alden called out to his men, who had already begun the congratulatory merriment.

Before the sunrise, Jacob and Alden returned to the laboratory and lit one lantern. Each held one corked bottle. Jacob held the Philosopher's Stone as Alden held the essence of the lodestone.

"I believe you must open the Philosopher's Stone first. When we are safely enclosed in the field it creates, I will open the lodestone essence. Are you ready?"

"Yes, I am." Jacob unleashed the Philosopher's Stone. Once again, Jacob and Alden stood in the midst of an electric storm, safely cocooned in the middle. Alden then opened the bottle he held.

The storm intensified. Between the flashes of light, they watched as every piece of metal in the laboratory flew into the wall of energy with such force that the metal was completely and totally demolished.

Alden and Jacob corked their bottles. They stood in the now quiet and completely dark laboratory. The force they had created had ransacked the cellar. There was not one piece of metal left. All had been destroyed. However, Alden and

Jacob remained untouched by the ruble that had flown around them. They had been safely shielded inside the cocoon.

"Just as we thought, Jacob, we have created an extraordinarily strong electromagnet. We did not lose any of our elixirs, only the metal objects. Certainly the retort will be missed, but we will bear up. I could not have done it without you."

"This is good, very good, Alden. We have worked together and we have succeeded. We will be able to protect the channel."

"Yes, Jacob, we have been successful. But we must not be too hasty. We first must test the boundaries and the strength before we can know its true power."

Two days later, all of Jacobs's and Alden's men stood in Lord Smithe's hayfield one hundred meters from where Alden, Jacob, and Lord Smithe stood. Each of them held a large and very heavy piece of scrap metal, Alden began speaking.

"Thank you, Smithe, for joining us and for allowing us to use your field for our final test of the force."

Lord Smithe laughed. "Righty-o, Alden, I wouldn't miss this for all the gold in the king's crown! Keep calm and carry on."

Jacob opened his bottle, and the three men were immediately cocooned. Alden then opened his. Straight away, a storm of metal hit the cocoon with such magnitude that the ground measurably shook. Once again, every piece of metal that slammed into the wall of energy was obliterated, but the men were left unscathed.

"This is certainly impressive, but pieces of scrap do not equate the Kriegsmarine. The German navy will certainly be a more formidable foe than a few scraps of rubbish." Lord Smithe said. "I say, old chap, impressive nonetheless, but what say you tell your men to harness six of my draft horses to the reaper and lead them no farther than fifty meters from the point where we stand."

The men did as Smithe said. Once more Jacob opened the Elixir of the Philosopher's stone and then Alden followed with the elixir of loadstone. The force surrounded the three men, the reaper rumbled, and the horses spooked as the reaper, and the horses left the ground. The reaper and the horses hopelessly entangled in their harness were swiftly and assuredly dashed to their destruction. Not one piece of the horses' carcass or a scrap of the reaper remained.

"Well, I dare say that was a bloody surprise. I never expected the force would move the reaper, much less the reaper *and* the horses." Smithe, looked to Alden and then to Jacob. "I say chaps, had you an inkling the force was this stalwart?"

Alden's face had paled, his mouth hung open he stuttered. "We… We knew it would be formidable but we could not have known the extent."

"I am sorry for the loss of your magnificent animals Lord Smithe." Jacob hung his head.

"Yes, yes, sad indeed. Jacob, but stiff upper lip you know." Smithe drew on his personal strength, and carried on. "I say Alden; all that is left of this endeavor will be to establish when the Kriegsmarine is moving. I have a contact; I will get back with you chaps when I have news. Keep calm and carry on."

Smithe left the men and returned to his manor. The men spent the rest of the day in the hayfield combing it for scraps of metal that had escaped complete destruction. None were found the men finally retired to the barn. The tired and hungry men congratulated one another on the day's work well done as they enjoyed the pot of stew Lydia had left them.

The sound of dogs barking in the night alerted Clarisse to activity in the street. From her window, she could see someone walking toward the edge of the village. Clarisse quickly dressed and rushed from her home, past the edge of the village, and into the forest. Yet, she was unable to catch the person before they disappeared into the shadows.

She turned back toward the village and walked only a short distance when she caught sight of a sudden bright light. Clarisse turned and ran through the brush toward the light; smoke caught her breath as she neared the source. She found herself standing in front of Lord Smithe's barn. A fire was blazing around the foundation and leaping up the walls.

She looked to the roof of the barn. The bay window was open. The huge, silent man who accompanied Alden and Jacob to the market stood at the bay, his eyes fixed on her.

She called out to him, "FIRE! WARN THE

OTHERS!" Then, she disappeared into the forest.

Auvil knelt beside Jacob. "Fire," Auvil spoke. The word reverberated as if it echoed back from the uttermost regions of the earth.

Jacob sprang to his feet. Smoke filled the barn. The men called out in search of their comrades as the flames engulfed the lower level and now threatened the supports that held the loft. Alden gathered the elixirs from the chest they were hidden in. He secured the precious elixirs on his person then he called to the men who were still in the burning barn.

"The bay window! The rope!" Alden yelled over the roar of the flames. The men escaped certain death as they dropped to the ground.

Once on the ground, Jacob and Alden accounted for all of their men, save for Bertram the elder and Belenus the golem.

The fire hissed and writhed before them. Flames slithered up the sides of the barn and threatened to sting even the night sky. Then, from the belly of the blazing serpent, Belenus arose, Bertram cradled in his massive arms. Belenus gently laid the old Alchemist on the ground at Alden's feet.

"Thank you, Belenus. You have done well. We will see to him now." Alden knelt beside Bertram's body and wept the loss of his elder and cherished friend.

With his water wagon, Lord Smithe was able only to prevent the fire from spreading to the forest. The barn was lost. However, the laboratory deep underground beneath the stone foundation of the barn still held its secrets. Jacob stationed Belenus in the dark cellar to guard the contents of the laboratory. Jacob then instructed the golem, "Belenus, listen and obey. This laboratory is in your keep. Watch and protect it. Act only if there is a threat."

Jacob left the cellar and joined Alden, Lord Smithe, and the rest of the men as they laid   Bertram to rest beneath the large evergreen that has long stood between the forest and the edge of the road. The grand and aged tree has marked the countryside for so many years that it has become a journeyman's point of reference.

"Alden, you and the men will come and stay in the manor until this is over. You may set up a makeshift laboratory in my basement," Lord Smithe said. The exhausted men trudged into the breaking dawn to Lord Smithe's manor.

There was no argument the men would be the guests of
Smithe for the duration.

From the forest's deep shadows a figure appeared.
Lydia stood among the smoldering ashes. She muttered as she
poked through the ruins.

"I must make certain that all is destroyed for the
Fatherland."

As she searched she discovered a secreted set of stone
steps that led to a room hidden deep beneath the barn. Lydia
used her flashlight to light the steps that led into the darkness.
There in the cellar she discovered the Alchemist's laboratory,
the object of her destruction was still intact.

Lydia did not notice the fierce guardian that stood
in the shadows. She placed her light on the table it afforded
enough illumination for her to act. Lydia picked one beaker
from the shelf and threw it against the wall and then another
followed by a corked bottle. Lydia reached for another bottle.
A vice-like hand gripped her arm, shattering her bone. Lydia
screamed. Belenus had silently crept behind her. Belenus
picked her up by the back of her jacket and smashed her
against the stone wall. The power with which he forced

her into the wall was such that his massive hand penetrated through her thorax. Most of Lydia fell at once, but bits and pieces of Lydia slowly followed the slimy visceral trail down the wall to finally join her on the cold cellar floor.

Lord Smithe sat in his library with his guest. They whispered as they sipped their afternoon tea.

"You remember Lydia, the young woman from the village? We found her dead in the laboratory," Smithe said.

"Lydia? What happened?"

"Do you fancy the truth or the official story?"

"I would like to hear both, Smithe."

"We charred her body and told her father that she was somehow caught up in the fire. However, the truth is the golem that was guarding the laboratory killed her. She was destroying the laboratory. We found some papers on her. Seems she was following orders."

"So she was a Nazi."

"Yes and a dangerous one at that. Now, I must ask you a favor. The men have finished their work. We need information from your contact in the Kriegsmarine."

"What information do you need from the Nazis' war navy?"

"We need to know when the war ships are moving toward the channel. Upon that information the men will boat into the channel and set the force of our resistance."

"They think this force they have will be effective?"

"The Nazis' entire war navy cannot penetrate the force they have created."

"Very well, Smithe. You will have your information."

"Thank you, Clarisse. Would you care for another spot of tea?"

Clarisse smiled. "Why, yes, Smithe, I certainly would."

More than a year had passed since Jacob and his men reach England. It was more time than Jacob cared to mark. The full moon had drawn him out of his slumber. On this cold November night he sat in the hushed meadow. It was November the ninth, the night of Jacobs's fitful remembrances. The night of the broken glass, the night he last held his precious Sara Rosa. This night he held a small vile in his hand and whispered, "Why do I go on mourning because of the oppression of the enemy?" A few drops of the Philosopher's Stone lay at the bottom of the corked bottle he held. He spoke to Auvil, who was sitting behind him.

"Tonight, Auvil, I open the elixir on my own." Jacob opened the bottle, inside the whirling cocoon his thoughts were of his precious Miriam. He implored the God of the universe for her protection.

CHAPTER TWELVE

THE MITER STAND

November 11, 2014

Doctor Sam's office manager's accent identifies her as a New York City native. Denise is not the typical New York transplant. Denise is most certainly not typical anything. She has been Doctor Sam's office manager for thirteen years. Only once in those thirteen years has a salesperson gotten past her by posing as a potential patient. The salesman had made an appointment for a consultation with the doctor. Denise now keeps a skimpy hospital gown in her desk drawer. If a persistent vendor or sales representative is willing to don the hospital gown, they may have a ten-minute consult with the doctor.

"Paul Linder is here to see you, Doctor Rubinstein,"

"Good, send him in, D."

"I'm Paul Linder. We spoke on the phone yesterday."

"You got here quickly, young man. Where did you say you are from? Ohio?"

"Indiana, sir."

"Yes, of course."

"Our computer spit out the police report on your Jane Doe. I'd like to see her." Paul's attention is focused on the two large watercolors on Doctor Sam's office wall.

"Longfield-Smith," Doctor Sam says.

"Pardon me?" Paul turns his attention back to the doctor.

"The artist, Longfield-Smith."

"They're very colorful, Doctor."

"She lived in Barbados in the early 1900s. She tried to capture the bright, carefree island life. When I was a boy, I dreamed of living on a lush tropical island. I guess that's what drew me to these two watercolors." Doctor Sam's memory lingers in the bleak days of the camp and his dreams of escape to a better place.

"I like them. My grandfather was an artist, not

famous, but he left some nice work behind."

Doctor Sam stares at the brightly colored pictures for a moment longer. Still to this day he plans his escape to a tropical paradise, but now his plans include his Leah, the wife of his youth.

"Yes, yes." Doctor Sam returns to the present and the mystery at hand. "The girl, what is the nature of your curiosity, young man?"

"Our computer monitors for any reports of crimes or activities that could be neo-Nazi or Aryan-Nation-related," Paul began. "The tattoo on her arm is what the computer picked up on. We investigate what comes up, and sometimes it leads us to old Nazi war criminals, the old ones who got away."

"I believe most of them are gone, by now young man. However if there are any left, I hope you bring them to justice."

"That's the plan, sir."

"I'm curious, Paul. What made you become a Nazi hunter?"

"My father and grandfather were Nazi hunters. My

grandfather died in South America chasing some pretty notorious ones. My father chased Nazis all around South Africa. I guess it's just what I'm wired for."

"Let's go down to ICU so you can see the girl, Paul." As they walk Paul is very much aware of the nurses who follow him with their eyes, admiring his ruggedly handsome good looks, while desiring his chiseled body, to consume upon their lust.

"She's not awake, but she's stable." Doctor Sam says as they enter the woman's room.

"Have you found out anything about her?" Paul steps to the woman's bedside.

"No, we have put out pictures. *The Trib* even did a human interest piece, but no one has come forward—just one old nun from Europe—but that turned out to be nothing."

Paul makes notes, studies the woman's tattoo and commits her face to memory. "Thank you for your time, Doctor. I want to get to my hotel now and see what will come up on the web. Might be a pattern, or something, you never know. Thanks again, Doctor. *Auf Wiedersehn.*"

"Do you speak German?"

"Only a little, I took it in school. My father was German. Tryin' to keep in touch with my heritage, ya know." Paul chuckles, his soft blue eyes sparkling.

"Very good." Doctor Sam accompanies Paul to the elevator. "Keep me posted, Paul. We can use your expertise."

"I'll be back." Paul does his best Schwarzenegger impersonation as the elevator doors close.

Doctor Sam heads to the cafeteria. He meets Doctor Knowles in the hall.

"David, do you have time to join me in the cafeteria?

"Sure, Sam, I have time."

"Have you checked in on Jane Doe yet today David?"

"I was in there earlier. It's a strange case."

"Well, you won't know anything for sure until you get the blood work." Doctor Sam wouldn't really deceive his friend, but leaving something out isn't lying, it's omitting. Until he knows what happened to this young woman, the lab reports which confirm the woman's drug-free status will remain locked in his drawer.

"What do you think, Sam?"

"I think she will wake up tomorrow or the next day.

But I've been wrong before." Doctor Sam smiles.

"I'll watch her closely. What's with the guy who was in the girl's room?"

"Big boy Nazi hunter. Not much to tell. We'll see. It was crazy last night. It must have been a full moon." Just as the doctors reach the cafeteria, Knowles' pager sounded.

"Guess we'll catch up another time. I got to go." Doctor Knowles hurried to the callbox.

"I'll see you tomorrow, David."

"Good afternoon, Doctor." Paul lays a manila folder on the doctor's desk.

"Please sit down."

"I researched Jane Doe's tattoo on the web last night. It turns out that it was actually given to a girl in 1940." Paul makes himself comfortable as he sits in the chair in front of Doctor Sam's desk.

"That is very interesting, Paul. But it could be a coincidence."

"There's more. The girl's name was Miriam Ruth Davidson. She was the daughter of Jacob Davidson, some kind of mystic Kabbalah person the Nazis were looking for. The girl escaped from the Gestapo when the vehicle she was being transported in was in an accident. She was lost in the forest and was presumed to be dead."

Doctor Sam raises his eyebrows. "How do you know all of this?"

Paul goes on. "The Nazis kept records of everything. It can be found on the web if you know how to get it. But there's more. The forest she was lost in was near the town that my grandfather was from in Germany, so I got online with my father. He, in turn, searched my grandfather's records and came up with this."

Paul takes a copy of a hand-drawn sketch from the folder that he had laid on Doctor Sam's desk. A sentence is printed in German across the top of the paper.

"'We are searching for this woman.'" Doctor Sam reads the words out loud.

"Don't you see the resemblance, Doctor? I think the girl in Germany didn't die in the forest, and I think this woman is a relative of that girl."

"Tell me how your grandfather came across this

paper."

"My grandfather made this sketch. He was a member of the German resistance, the Miter Stand. He went undercover and gained the Nazis trust. They thought he was just a big deaf fool, so they were never careful of what they said in front of him."

"They were brave men, the Miter Stand. May I keep this copy?"

"Yes, of course. I had hoped to be able to talk to Jane Doe, but something has come up at home, something we've been working on for a while. I'll be leaving this afternoon, but may I come back?"

"We will look forward to it, and I'll let you know if I find anything more. Sam locks the sketch in his desk drawer along with the lab reports.

The events of the last few days have flooded Doctor Sam's mind with memories of hiding from the Gestapo. Memories of moving with his mother from one cellar to the next, hiding in attics, secret rooms, churches, or monasteries, trying to escape Nazi Germany and of traveling the underground until they could reunite with his father, a "mystic Kabbalah person," as Paul had put it.

"Doctor Sam, Doctor Knowles is on line one."

"Thanks, D. put him through. What can I do for you, David?"

"I'll be down in ER for a while. Can you check on Jane Doe for me?"

"Certainly David, I was just on my way down there."

"Thanks, Doc."

"Miriam?" Doctor Sam tries the name that Paul left with him. "Miriam Davidson?"

The woman's eyelids flutter. Doctor Sam takes her hand, she opens her eyes. The young woman stares at the old doctor sitting next to her bed, but says nothing.

"You're in the hospital. You have been badly hurt, but you're going to be all right," Sam says quietly. He wets the corner of a clean cloth with cold water and gently touches it to her lips.

"You have a visitor." Doctor Sam smiles. He points to the raven at the window.

"Sandalphon," she whispers as she closes her eyes.

215

Doctor Sam quietly leaves the young woman sleeping. He stops at the nurses' station and gives explicit instructions.

"Jane Doe is awake. I want you to check on her every twenty minutes. No sudden moves or loud noises. She's fragile. Do not wake her if she is sleeping. Quietly reassure her if she is awake. Do not question her. If she says she is hungry, give her clear liquid. Thank you, nurse." Doctor Sam returns to his office and dials his home.

"Hello, Leah. I won't be home tonight. Jane Doe woke up. I want to talk with her as soon as she is able. I love you, darling. Good night."

"I thought this was your day off, David." Doctor Sam looks up from studying the nurse's notes. Morning rounds seldom found Doctor Sam on duty, but this morning he has been in ICU since dawn.

"I'm not officially here. Just thought I'd check on Jane before I take off. Bicycling today" David grinned.

"Not much change since she woke up last night. I stayed in case she woke up. I'll let you know if something happens. Go, David. Go and enjoy your day."

"Okay. I really need this day off. I need to ride, Thanks, Sam."

"Enough. Go ride your bicycle before I change my mind."

"You have my cell number, right?"

"Yes. Now, for the last time, go." With that, David Knowles hurries from the room.

The woman opens her eyes and stares at the ceiling.

"Good morning, young lady. We've been waiting for you. I'm Doctor Rubinstein."

The woman glances at Doctor Sam and then returns her gaze to the ceiling.

"How are you feeling this morning?"

"You are German," she whispers.

"Yes, I am. I suspect by your accent that you are, too. Your friend, Sandalphon, is still at the window. He's been looking for you. He has been your guardian, just like the spirit."

"You know of Sandalphon?" the woman asks.

"The bird or the spirit, my dear?"

"The spirit."

"I only know what I have read in my father's Kabbalah."

"Your father's Kabbalah?" The woman winces as she attempts to move closer to the doctor. She looks around the room and leans closer.

"Do they force you to work here?" she whispers.

"Force me? Who? I don't understand, dear."

"I apologize. I have used the wrong words."

"It's all right. Tell me about yourself." Doctor Sam holds the woman's hand as he speaks.

"They have not told you?"

"No, no one knows anything to tell about you."

"Of course they know. They brought me here. They must have told you." The woman pulls her hand away.

"Who are 'they'? Who are you afraid of?"

"The Gestapo," she whispers as she closed her eyes.

"Gestapo." Even now, after all the years, the word returns Samuel Rubinstein to a little boy's world of fear. He sees that same fear reflected in this woman's eyes.

"My head hurts," she mumbles.

"You have a concussion. You've been unconscious for

four days."

"Did a very old sister come to my room, or was I dreaming? Four days? Then, it is the thirteenth of November?"

"Yes, the thirteenth. Is there someone you would like me to call?"

"Call?"

"Call. Contact your family or a friend."

"Do you mean my father?"

"Yes, can I contact him?"

"I told them I do not know where he is and that I do not know what he can do. I will tell you the same. You can send me back but I cannot tell you what I do not know."

Suddenly, Paul's words come back to Doctor Sam. Miriam believes she is the daughter of a Jewish mystic.

"I'd like to show you something." He pushes the sleeve of his lab coat far enough up his arm to reveal his tattoo. "This tattoo was my identification. The tattoo on your arm was given to a young girl. Her name was Miriam Davidson. Are you related to her?"

"Why do you say you know nothing of me and then

219

say my name?"

"So your name is Miriam Davidson also?"

"Is there another Miriam Davidson here?"

"No, I'm referring to the Miriam Davidson who was presumed dead after an accident that occurred while she was being transported to a detainment center."

"I am Miriam Ruth Davidson. I am not dead. I do not know where my father and the others are. I do not know about the Kabbalah or what my father can or cannot do." Her eyes fluttered. "I am tired." The woman closes her eyes and gives in to a medicated sleep.

Doctor Sam studies the young woman. She is convinced that she is Miriam Ruth Davidson, the young girl who died more than sixty years ago. Miriam Ruth. How does she know the woman's middle name? Doctor Sam is sure he had not used it. It is very possible she had gotten the name and the other information from the web, just the same as Paul Linder had, but a small quiet voice whispers, "Listen with your heart."

CHAPTER THIRTEEN

THE WEB

Doctor Sam helped Sister Theresa Marie to a comfortable chair.

"Thank you for coming, Sister. You must be very busy setting up the display of religious antiquity. There's been quite a write up about it in *The Trib*."

"We have been *very* busy. We have only two months to get the religious treasures and the icons ready for the seventy-fifth anniversary celebration of the Holy Trinity, so I don't have much time to spend."

"Would you like a cup of tea?"

"Tea would be nice. Thank you. Now tell me, how I may help you?"

Doctor Sam sets the cup in front of Sister Theresa Marie. "Sister, you told the officer that you don't know the young woman you visited. You said she reminded you of someone. Can you tell me about that person?"

"That was so many years ago in Germany. It was a dark time in our history." The nun sips her tea.

"Yes, a dark time, Sister, a very dark time indeed. It was only for the courage of many like you that some survived. Tell me what you can about that woman, Sister."

Sister Theresa Marie is quiet for a moment, she removes her glasses and dries the corner of her eyes.

"A day has not passed that I have not said a prayer for her. The person I knew was just a young woman, no more than a girl really. She was brought to our monastery by her father. He hoped to hide her with us from the Gestapo. We were successful in hiding her for more than a year, and then she was discovered and taken away. I never saw her again. It was rumored she had escaped, but I assumed she died in a camp."

"Can you tell me anything about her?" Doctor Sam asks. "Do you know if she had family or friends, a pet or maybe you remember her family name? Can you remember anything about that girl anything, even if it seems insignificant, Sister?"

Sister Theresa Marie searches her memories. "Yes, a pet. I remember she found a bird while she was with us, a raven. She called him Sandalphon. It was so long ago. This is all that I recall. I am very old you know." The Sister smiles slyly. "The memory fades." Sister Theresa Marie shakes the memories from her head. "Doctor, I must return to the monastery. I have much to do. I'm sorry I could not help you."

"Thank you again, Sister." Doctor Sam escorted the sister to the door and then turned to Denise.

"D, get me Paul Linder on the phone please."

"You got something?"

"I think so."

Sister Theresa Marie's words—"rumored she had escaped," "a raven she called him Sandalphon"—are racing through Doctor Sam's head when the phone rings. "Hello, Paul. It's Sam from Tampa. I have a quick question. Are there any details about Miriam Davidson online, anything about a pet?"

"I didn't see anything about it when I was going

through, but let me look. I'm right by a computer. Can I put you on hold for a few minutes?"

"Great. Yes, I can hold."

"I'm sorry Doctor Sam there's nothing that I could find. I can look again for you next time I research."

"No, that's probably good, Paul. Anyway, it was just a hunch." Sam walked out to D's office. "I'm going down to Jane Doe. Hold my calls please, D."

"You're awake. How are you feeling? Hungry?" Doctor Sam pulls a chair next to Jane Doe's bed.

"Yes, hungry."

"I'll have the nurse bring you something to eat. Does your head still hurt?"

"Not as much."

Tap, tap, tap

Doctor Sam looked to the window. "Sandalphon tapped for you the whole time you were unconscious. I have never known anyone with a pet raven. Did you find him?"

"He found me."

"Sandalphon...you named him after the spirit on

Jacob's ladder."

"I know nothing of Jacob's ladder."

"I didn't know very much about the spirit world or the Kabbalah when the Gestapo took me. I was too young to study Kabbalah, but of course, the Nazis didn't know that. I survived because I told them the little that I knew in bits over the years and made up the rest."

"What do you mean you were too young?"

"I was only six years old when the Gestapo found us and took me from my mother. I'll never forget the day. The soldiers separated me from my mother, but I ran away from them and fought my way back to her. As the soldiers pulled me away again, she whispered in my ear, 'It is better to be a living dog than a dead lion.' I did not see her again until the camps were liberated in forty-five."

"Forty-five, forty-five what?"

"In 1945. I was eight years old. I was in the camp from 1943 to 1945. Two years."

"Doctor, what you are telling me is nonsense. You could not be eight years old in 1945 when it is November 13, 1940 today!"

"1940? My dear, this is November 13, *2014.*"

"Time! Jacob's ladder…" she whispers, "Sandalphon the spirit. Doctor, my father was right. The ladder is a door." Miriam's eyes widen as she speaks.

"Don't be afraid, child,"

"I am not afraid, Doctor, I gained knowledge from my father's journal, and with knowledge must come understanding. Sandalphon the spirit has allowed me passage through a spirit door, through time, and so may it be." Miriam closes her eyes and envisioned Jacob's ladder and time spiraling through the spirit realm.

"Mike DeAugustino is here, Doctor. He's asking to talk to the patient." The nurse had been true to her word and alerted Mike when Jane Doe awoke.

"One minute, nurse."

Doctor Sam leans close to Miriam and whispers to her in German.

"Listen to me, child. My heart tells me that you are telling the truth and you have somehow come here upon Jacob's ladder. I will help you, but you must say that you don't remember anything. You must say that to anyone who

226

questions you. Can you do that?"

"Ja, I will." she whispers.

Mike knocks on the side of the door and enters the room. "Doctor, can I talk to her now?"

"Yes, but she seems to be suffering from amnesia. She's still weak. You can have only a few minutes."

"How are you feeling? You look better than you did when we found you." Mike smiles.

"My head hurts. You found me?"

"Yeah, me and my partner found you."

"You are police?"

"Yes, can you answer a few questions for me?" Mike opens his note pad. "What is your name?"

"I do not know."

"Can you tell me who did this to you?"

"No, I do not know. I do not remember."

"Where do you live?"

Miriam looks to Doctor Sam and then to Mike. "I do not know."

"Mike, I think that's all for now. She's had enough for today." Doctor Sam interrupts. He walks with Mike into the hall.

"Do you think she's faking?" Mike asks once they were in the hall.

"I don't think so, Mike. I've seen this before. Severe trauma, whether physical or emotional, can cause the mind to shut down. We'll have her evaluated in a day or so if she doesn't snap out of it."

"Thanks, Doc. I'm going to close this case for now. I can't prove a crime was committed if she doesn't remember. Call me if she remembers anything."

"He's real scared, Vicky. He's all I got." Joniqua is talking quietly with Vicky in the hospital's parking garage.

Mike and Vicky were in agreement that a certain amount of contact with the street people was helpful, but Mike is not supportive of her involvement with Joniqua. He has tried to explain to Vicky that although Joniqua was probably harmless, the people she hangs with certainly were not. At the sight of Mike, Joniqua stops talking and watches him get into the patrol car. Mike sounds two short blasts of the siren, and grins at Vicky.

"I'll see what I can do. I promise." Vicky glares at Mike as she walks to the car.

"Click it or ticket. Buckle up. I'd hate to ticket you. What were the scrubs about, some new hook?"

"Joniqua said she's been off the streets for months. She's been going to the annex for some nursing courses. She'll be finished soon. She's interning now. And, Mike, you better never sound that siren at me again, hear?" Vicky will not have to tell him again.

"Sorry. What did you promise?" Mike mumbles.

"Joniqua's son knows something about the boy who was murdered over on Channel Side."

"Did she say that?"

"She said some stuff about drugs and gangs. No details. She wants help, protection for her son in exchange for information." Vicky pinches the soft skin behind her ear and worries as she watches the streets of Tampa whiz by.

"Don't worry, Vic. We'll keep your promise. It'll be okay."

"Thanks, Mike. What happened with Jane Doe?"

"Amnesia, according to the doctor."

"Amnesia? Baloney skin on the pump handle," Vicky declares.

"Well, the doctor says so. I closed the case for now, but you know it as well as I do, something just isn't right."

"Miriam, can you tell me the last thing you remember?" Doctor Sam whispers.

"I was in the back of a truck. The soldiers were taking me somewhere. My head hurt. I dreamed of my father and Jacob's ladder spinning in time and remembered what my father had written in his journal. He thought the ladder was a door to the spirit realm. He thought that there are many doors that open to the spirit realm. My head hurt so badly I could hardly think. I wanted to escape, so I drew in chalk on the floor of the truck. I drew Jacob's ladder as it is drawn in the Kabbalah. I knew that I could not escape, so I decided that if I could not escape, I would rather die than go where they were taking me. I cut deep into my wrist and laid myself on the chalk ladder. When I woke up, it was morning, and I was sitting on a bench. Where am I, Doctor?"

"Somehow, Miriam, you did open a door or ladder,"

230

Doctor Sam says. "You're in Tampa, Florida, my dear, America. But I don't know why you are here, or why you came at this time."

"America?! I have been brought across time and distance to be here."

"I wonder why your bird is here."

"He was lying next to me. When I was brought up, I suppose he was carried along. There is a purpose, Doctor. Although I do not know it yet, this existence shall be revealed in its time. What will we do until the reason is known?"

"Between your guardian Sandalphon and me, your friend, we'll think of something. Try to get some sleep now."

"Doctor?"

"Yes?"

"You did not answer my question. Did an old sister come to my room?"

"Yes, she did."

"Will she come back?

"If you like, I will see to it. Rest now, child."

"Yes, I would like that." Miriam closes her eyes.

Doctor Sam sits at the computer in his office. He is not a computer genius, but he has skills. He can scan a document, alter it, print it, and then he can fax it. Yes, the old doctor has skills. Doctor Knowles will have Jane Doe's bogus lab reports on his desk in the morning.

CHAPTER FOURTEEN

BUREAUCRACY

The telephone is ringing as Doctor Sam unlocks his office door. "Doctor Rubinstein here."

"Good morning, Sam."

"Ah, good morning, David."

"I got the labs you faxed over. Rohypnol, a big dose!"

"She's lucky to be alive." *Not a lie*, Doctor Sam thought.

"Strange that there was no alcohol involved."

"Hmm, I didn't think of that."

"She might have been the designated driver. She could have gotten it in a soda or something," David said.

"A lot of unanswered questions, David. Have you had a chance to talk to her?"

"This morning, I talked to her a little. I didn't get anywhere. What do you think, Doc?"

"I think we'll get a specialist in a day or so."

"Shouldn't we get someone in sooner?"

"No, David, I think she needs a little more time. I'll go down this afternoon. I promised her that I would help her."

"Who are you going to ask to see her? Kline? He's the best."

"I was thinking about Boyd. Kline's too opinionated."

"Boyd? He's a moron." David is surprised at Sam's choice of residents.

"Boyd's a good man. Give him a chance, David. Oh, and have her transferred to a private room tomorrow." Sam knows David's assessment of Doctor Boyd's medical skills is more than accurate, but Boyd will suit his purpose.

"Okay, Sam, if you think he's the man, it's all right with me. I'll talk to you later."

"David, wait, will you do a favor for me?"

"Sure. What is it?"

"I need you to get with maintenance and give them a work order to remove the television from the room you put

Jane Doe in."

"All right, Sam, but why?"

"The woman is fragile, and I don't want her exposed to any excess stimuli."

"Good call."

"Thanks, David." Doctor Sam's good call also covers the fact that he does not want Miriam exposed to any information that might begin to bring her up to speed with the twenty-first century before her sessions with Doctor Boyd.

The hospital room is lit only by the streams of light that shine through the partially closed mini blinds. Sandalphon remains perched on the ledge, guarding his keep.

"Good afternoon, young lady." Doctor Sam says.

"Doctor, what is going to happen to me now?" Miriam asks.

"I told you that I will help you. Don't worry. I have a plan. All you will have to do is play dumb."

"Excuse me? Play dumb?"

"Just an expression I'm going to bring a specialist in to examine you."

"What is a specialist?"

"A doctor who is an expert in a certain field."

"What will this doctor do to me?"

"The doctor I am bringing will ask you questions about yourself," Doctor Sam explained. "You must remember to answer that you do not remember anything to each of his questions.

"I must tell the doctor that I do not remember?"

"Do you think you can do that, just like you did with the police officer?"

"Ja, but then what?"

"Then I will suggest to the doctor that he hypnotize you."

"Hypnotize? I have never been hypnotized. Will it hurt?" Miriam is puzzled.

"No child, I won't let anyone hurt you. He will just talk to you until you relax. Then he will ask you questions. It will be alright, just answer his questions. Trust me, it will all work out."

"I know it will work out, Doctor. I have been brought here for a reason. Thank you."

Doctor Samuel Rubinstein, will you please go to the nearest call box?"

"I'm being paged, I'll be back soon. Just remember, don't worry, child." Doctor Sam hurries to the call box.

"Yes, Denise?"

"I'm sorry to bother you, but there are some men here. I think they're from the government," Denise whispers into the phone.

"It's all right, D. Tell them I'll be right there."

Doctor Sam knew that there would be an official investigation, what with all the safeguards that have been put in place in the years since 9/11, but the doctor's plan covers Homeland Security, too. If it all goes as planned, Miriam will be deemed an amnesiac, not a threat to national security. She will be monitored for a time, and eventually, her case will be filed away and forgotten. The Feds are waiting in his office; now he has to pull this plan together.

"This is it," Doctor Sam whispers as he opened the door to his office. "You can do this."

"Good afternoon. I'm Doctor Rubinstein."

"Good afternoon, Doctor. I'm Agent Broadstreet,

and this is Agent Giles." Giles stands a few inches behind Broadstreet who almost eclipses the smaller, baby-faced man. Their stance is reminiscent of an offensive player protecting his quarterback in the pocket.

"How can I help you?" Doctor Sam asks.

"We need to fingerprint your Jane Doe and take some pictures so that we can run a background on her."

"The girl is very fragile right now. I can't allow you to stress my patient."

"We respect that, but this woman has just appeared from nowhere with no identification of any kind and supposedly no memory. We must be allowed to investigate her." Broadstreet's finger ringed the size-eighteen collar of his starched, white shirt, trying in vain to relieve the pressure that the collar and the double-knotted black necktie bear on his size-nineteen neck.

"She could be a citizen, and if she is, she has rights whether she remembers those rights or not. I'm certain you will also respect that possibility."

"Of course, Doctor, we're here to protect the citizens. All we want to know is if the woman has any terrorist connections."

"I can allow you to do this, but I only ask that you do not interrogate her at this time. If you find something during your investigation that is deemed a threat though, of course, I understand that you will have to act. Come, I'll take you to her."

The men follow Doctor Sam, to Miriam's room where they take her fingerprints and photographs. Broadstreet pays special attention to the tattoo on her arm. When they are done, Broadstreet and Giles keep their word to Doctor Sam and quietly leave.

"Who were those men?" Miriam asks.

"They're from the government. They are trying to find out who you are."

"How can they know?"

"They can't. They'll find nothing. Don't worry."

"Doctor?"

"Yes?"

"Will the old sister come back?"

"Yes, child, she will. Rest now." Doctor Sam walks to the door.

"Doctor?

"Yes, dear?"

"Thank you." Miriam closes her eyes.

Doctor Sam's office is quiet. Denise is on her lunch break. She is a good office manager, and over the years, she has become a good friend. Denise watches over her friend Sam like a gruff and temperamental mama bear. However if the brusque bear mantle were stripped away a beautiful, fragile and delicate bird would be revealed to the world.

Doctor Sam has a few minutes to himself before the caseworker's appointment; Social Services will be the last hurdle to mount before Miriam is out of the woods.

"I have a good plan. All my *I's* are dotted, and *T's* crossed. This will work. You've been doing this long enough to know how to work it," Doctor Sam says to himself. He answers the knock on his office door.

"Doctor? I'm Ms. Johnson from Social Services."

"Good afternoon Ms. Johnson." Doctor Sam greets the young woman.

Ms. Johnson has the most beautiful, biggest brown

eyes that Samuel Rubinstein has ever seen. Although she may be considered mousy by the world's unrealistic standards, Doctor Samuel Rubinstein is certain Ms. Johnson holds many a young man's attention.

"Ms. Johnson. Please come in, sit down." Doctor Sam directs her to the chair in front of his desk.

"Thank you, Doctor. I would like to address the Jane Doe case. I need some information for our review."

"Yes, Ms. Johnson, the young woman was brought in by the EMTs four days ago. As you know, HIPAA does not allow me to disclose anything about her medical condition."

"Of course, Doctor, but I need to get a sense of how long she will be in the hospital on state-provided assistance. I also will have to place her if she is unable to care for herself."

"She will be examined by one of our staff psychiatrists tomorrow. I assure you we will have a report for you within a day or two, Ms. Johnson."

"All right, Doctor, that sounds good. We're so swamped down at the department. There are so many cases and just too few case workers. Your help is really appreciated."

"I'll get in touch with you when we have a report, Ms. Johnson. Like I said, probably a day or two."

"Thank you Doctor. I will expect your call then."

"Yes, thank you, Ms. Johnson."

Doctor Sam sits at his desk and considers what needs to be accomplished in two days to satisfy the Social Services, Ms. Johnson, and the government. He has only two days. Two days is not much time, but it seems to the doctor that time is certainly on Miriam's side.

"D, I'm going down to ICU, and then I'm going home."

"Okay, Doctor, see you tomorrow."

"Yes, D, see you tomorrow."

CHAPTER FIFTEEN

A MATTER OF IMPORTANCE

Boyd Douglas Boyd waits at Doctor Sam's office door. What were his parents thinking? Certainly the young man had entered the mental health field to find the answer to that question and a myriad of other personal idiocy. He knocks softly on Doctor Sam's office door.

"Ah, Boyd, just the man I want to see. Come in, sit down."

"Sam, I just went down to the, uh, ICU to see your Jane Doe, but she wasn't there. Uh, what should I do?" Doctor Boyd tries to keep his distress from reflecting in his voice, but the pitch, cracks, and stumbles make him sound like either a very distraught thirty-year-old or a lovesick adolescent.

"David put her in a private room this morning. Usually, the nurses have that kind of information." Now, Sam is sure he has chosen the right man for the job.

"I know. Uh, they were all busy. Figured I'd take this time to come up and get your thoughts. What's going on with her?"

"Well, I'm glad you asked me. I've talked with her a few times. She's very young. I don't believe she is even twenty. I would guess eighteen or nineteen. There's physical trauma: cuts, bruises, and burns—looks like cigarette burns. She has a concussion, which could be the major factor of her memory loss, but there could be psychological factors also. I think that if she were my patient, I would ask her some questions and then hypnotize her to see if anything that she's blocked comes out," Doctor Sam slyly advises.

"Should…should I do that right away?" Boyd is clueless.

"You might want to see her a few times. You know, form a trust bond with the patient." Doctor Sam is spoon feeding the young Boyd. This is working out perfectly.

"I would like to start soon, maybe today. What do you

244

think, Sam?"

"Excellent. That is exactly what I would do. You're a good man, Boyd."

Doctor Sam stands, shakes Boyd's hand, gives him a hearty pat on the back, and walks him to the door. Sam sits back down at his desk. He is tired. The events of the last week have exhausted him, but he will continue. Doctor Sam has a vision to see this young woman through the immediate future. Then the distant future will have to take care of itself. Sam doesn't know why or exactly how this woman has come to him, but he knows it was not a mistake. There are no mistakes.

"D, I need to talk to one of the police officers who came in with Jane Doe. Her name is Vicky. Do you think you can get her on the phone for me? Please ask her to come in to my office at her earliest convenience."

"No problem, Doctor. I'll get back to you with that. Doctor Knowles just walked in. Do you have time to see him?"

"Of course, always. Send him right in, D."

Doctor Knowles takes the seat directly in front of

Doctor Sam's desk.

"What brings you here, David?"

"Boyd." David is concerned about the choice Doctor Sam made.

"What about Boyd? He just left here a short time ago." Sam sits down at his desk.

"Has he seen Jane Doe yet?"

"That's where he was heading when he left."

David leans toward his old mentor.

"Do you really think Boyd can handle this, Sam? I know you're usually right about things, but I'm concerned about this one." This is the first time David has ever questioned Sam's judgment.

"I see that you're concerned, David, but don't worry, I spoke extensively to him. He is a brilliant hypnotist, and we agree completely on his plan of treatment."

"Sam, I've seen amazing hypnotists in nightclub acts and carnival side shows. I don't know, but that says to me that one doesn't have to be a brilliant physician to make someone think they're a chicken."

"Don't worry, David. I'll be there observing. Nobody

will think they're a chicken." Sam chuckles. "As a matter of fact, I was just going down there when you came in. Come with me, if you like."

"No, I can't, but I feel better knowing that you will be there. I have to run now. Thanks, Sam." David hurries out of Sam's office, slightly embarrassed that he questioned his old friend.

Doctor Sam stops at Denise's desk.

"When you get Ms. Knight on the phone, will you ask her to please come in to my office? I must speak to her about a matter of great importance."

"Yes, Doctor. Anything I should know about?"

"Soon, Denise, soon."

"Hello, Doctor," Vicky says as she takes a seat in front of Doctor Sam's desk. "Your secretary called and told me that you have an important matter to discuss with me."

Doctor Sam smiles and nods. "I'm glad you could come right away."

"Well, I had the day off, so I came right in. What do you need to talk to me about, Doctor?"

"Our Jane Doe. You know that I fully support you and your efforts with the women who are occasionally brought here, and I wanted to talk to you about that."

"I don't understand what that has to do with Jane Doe, Doctor."

"I know that the ladies that you have been involved with, often because of your hard work, leave the streets and go on to more acceptable employment. You know that on your request, I have even given a few of the women you help my recommendations for their employment in this very hospital."

"Yes, I do know that Doctor, and I'm very thankful to you for what you've done. I know you wouldn't have called me here without a good reason, but I still don't know what that has to do with Jane Doe."

"Our Jane Doe, yes, yes. I know. I know I must come to the point." The doctor paces as he speaks. "She is here because… she came… it was a force." Doctor Sam continues pacing. Vicky looks confused as the old doctor paces about. "There is a point, but I can't really tell you anything about her except that *I know that I know you can help her.* Honestly,

Ms. Knight, I don't know why she's here or how exactly she came to be here. All I know is that she is a young girl who desperately needs help."

"Wow, I can't believe that you said *'I know that I know.'*" A smile stretches across Vicky's face. "I haven't heard anyone use that expression since my grandmother passed. Whenever she said, 'I know that I know,' well, no one questioned her after that. What do you need me to do, Doctor?" Vicky's mind races back to her grandmother, a mild unassuming woman, who in Vicky's estimation knew the secret of all the secrets.

"I'll tell you, Ms. Knight, if any young girl ever needed your help, this one certainly does. She needs a friend and quickly. I know it's a lot to ask you, and I understand if you can't help."

"I don't know how I would be able to help, and what about her memory? Does she remember anything, Doctor? Anything at all?"

"I can't say that she has any recollections, and Social Services want to place her since no one has identified her and she can't identify herself. Although I can tell you I am sure an institution is the wrong place for her."

"What do they expect?"

"They want her to have a place to live and employment when she is able."

"Well, that's not unusual."

"What I'm trying to tell you is she will be placed in an institution until they feel she is able to take care of herself if she doesn't have work and family or a friend to help. I'm going to give her a job, filing in my office, but I have no place for her to live and no guardian." Doctor Sam takes a breath and continues. "My hope is that you can help with that. There's not much more that I can tell you about this girl except I promise you that she's not a danger to you or herself. For the time being, I will just say she is lost in this world, and if you can accept that, I know that we will be able to help her find herself. Can you accept that?"

Doctor Sam stops pacing and looks at Vicky. He said what he had to say, and now he hopes for the best. Vicky looks back at him, long and hard.

"Let me say, Doctor, I heard of you and your reputation as an excellent doctor and a good man even before the first time I ever came here, and then after I got to know you, I knew what I heard was true. You're a good man. And Doctor, please call me Vicky."

The doctor chuckles lightly. "Thank you, Vicky. You're very kind." The doctor took a chance. He put bet on Vicky's character, and now he hopes that she will not disappoint him, but she has not agreed just yet.

"Hold up a minute, before I say anything let me see if I understand exactly what you are asking of me. You want me to take guardianship over this young woman and bring her into my home—a girl who showed up out of the blue with no known family and no one coming forward to identify her or claim her as a friend or even an acquaintance. And you want me to commit to this for an unspecified amount of time, and the reason being for this is to keep her from going into a state institution because you know that you know it's the wrong place for her. Is that correct, Doctor?"

"Yes, I suppose that sums it up pretty well."

"I wouldn't be inclined to agree to this proposal, but I do have a nice guest room, and you and I have worked together a time or two before. So yes I'll agree, but I need some time to get things ready." Vicky's mind wanders home to her guest room. "Hmm, Peach would be nice. Yes I think I'll paint the guest room peach."

"Yes, peach, very nice my dear. Thank you so much, Vicky." Doctor Sam steps from behind his desk and vigorously shakes Vicky's hand. "You're a good woman."

"Oh, okay then, I guess it's settled then. When do I get to meet her?"

"I have another meeting with the social worker, and then I will explain to our Jane Doe what will happen. She will have a few more sessions with our resident psychiatrist, and then she'll be ready to be released to your custody. Give me a few days. Thank you, Vicky. Thank you. You're an extraordinary woman. I will call you in a few days."

"I will be looking for your call Doctor."

"Doctor Boyd, I see you're getting along with my favorite patient,"

"Yes, Doctor Knowles. We're just finishing for today. We'll have another session in the morning," Boyd calls over his shoulder as he leaves the room.

Doctor Knowles sits on the stool next to Miriam's bed and studies her chart while the young lady eats.

"Well, little lady, looks like you have your appetite back. You're doing very well. How do you feel?"

"Better, I think."

"That's good. I'd rather hear 'Better, I think' than 'Awful, I think.'" Doctor Knowles peeps over the chart at Miriam. She smiles. "Ha, I knew I could make you smile."

Miriam points to the door and grins as Doctor Sam walks in pushing a wheelchair.

"Well, there you go, I get a faint smile, and he gets a full-out grin. What do you make of that, Doctor Sam?"

"I think you and Doctor Boyd are monopolizing this young lady's time, so now I'm taking her out. We're going to the atrium right now. Will you join us, Doctor Knowles?" Doctor Sam knows his offer will be declined.

"Sorry, wish I could say yes, but duty calls." Doctor Knowles continues his rounds.

Doctor Sam parks Miriam's wheelchair in a shady spot.

"I've brought you a surprise." Doctor Sam waves

across the atrium and then excuses himself.

A small figure of a woman makes her way through the courtyard and stands in the shady spot where Miriam sits.

"Theresa Marie!" Miriam opens her arms. Theresa sits down on the bench beside Miriam.

"Mary Katherine, is it really you? Are you the girl I prayed for all of these years? How is this even possible? Where have you been? What has happened to you?" Theresa Marie tries to bring some logic to this completely illogical situation.

"Theresa, Yes it is me. I am the girl you ate cookies with so long ago. One cookie in each hand. Just the way we like."

"Mary Katherine it is you." The old sister holds the young woman as they weep tears of joy and confusion.

"Yes it is, and there is so much I must tell you, but first tell me, how did you find me?"

"I did not find you, Mary Katherine. The saints have brought us together. I am here only by chance to accompany a display of religious treasures that have been brought here to be displayed at the Holy Trinity Monastery."

"The Holy Trinity Monastery? The one Ignatius's brother Klaus built?"

"Yes. Ignatius will be here also. He'll celebrate mass for the anniversary of the monastery. He's a cardinal now."

"Ignatius! Theresa, he is a very evil man!"

Theresa averts her eyes from Miriam. "I know. I have always known."

"How could you know? Tell me how you know, Theresa."

"It was when Ignatius first arrived at our monastery," Sister Theresa Marie began. "He was a new priest. We passed in the halls as I went to the archives, and he went to his office. I was always cordial to him, but never anything more. One morning, he followed me into my office. He said he had something he thought that I would like to see. He asked me to come to the window. I could not imagine what I would see there that I had never seen before. I went to the window. Suddenly he clasped his hand over my mouth and pushed me to the floor. And then…he raped me. Afterward he told me if I told anyone, I could be assured that he knew men who would gladly make the same thing, or worse, happened to my little sister in Italy. I have remained silent to this day."

"Oh, Theresa, I'm so sorry."

Sister Theresa Marie remained emotionless. "It was a long time ago, Miriam. I have come to terms with the truth that because of his action, I will never be worthy."

Miriam searches her friend's eyes the sadness overwhelms her. Although Miriam can see that Theresa Marie has suffered much, she can also see that her friend's soul is unscathed.

"Theresa, I have known you as a friend, a sister, and a confidant. I would champion your character even to the highest heavens if need be, but there is no need, as your love and your dedication to your beliefs are your magnificence."

"Miriam. I should have told you before, but I feared that Ignatius would be true to his word, so for the sake of my little sister, I remained silent until now."

"Tell me, Theresa, What made you tell me of all this now?"

"I am surprised you ask me such a question."

"Why are you so surprised?"

"Just think, Miriam. Think of what has happened

to you, and look at the outcome. I see that fate has done its worst for you, but because you do not serve the blind god of fortune. Your God has given you a new life. You have been given a special gift, Miriam, like the saints."

"Well, Theresa, I do not think I will be canonized anytime soon, but that is a kind thing for you to say."

"I wish you could see yourself as I see you now. You are not the girl I knew, yet you are. I don't know how, and I can't explain it, but you are different...remade."

"I have been changed. You are right, Theresa. I have been changed." Miriam's thoughts go to the moment that she crossed into the spirit and the gift that the first spirit bestowed upon her. Miriam smiles. Theresa will never know, at least not in this life, the extent of that special gift. "Tell me, Theresa, when will Ignatius celebrate mass at the Holy Trinity?"

"Ignatius will be there the Sunday after the Thanksgiving celebration. That is a little more than a week from now."

"Good, I will attend, but tell no one about me. If anyone asks, say only that I have come from your convent in

Germany to help you with the treasures. Do you understand, Theresa?"

Sister Theresa Marie nods. "I understand. I will say nothing. Now, I have a surprise for *you*. Miriam, you have another old friend here... Eliakim. He came with the rest of the antiquities."

Miriam's smile widens. "Eliakim...perfect. We have much to talk about before that mass."

Miriam's room is dimly lit. The blinds are drawn to block the late afternoon sun. Doctor Boyd speaks to Miriam in a quiet, metered tone as Doctor Sam observes.

"Listen to my voice. You are standing at the edge of a beautiful pool. Do you see the pool?"

"Yes," Miriam says.

"I will begin to slowly count backward from ten. As I count, you will descend the steps into the pool. When I reach one, you will be totally immersed in the water and be completely comfortable. Do you understand?"

"Yes."

"Ten, you step into the pool. Nine, a warm tingling

sensation covers your feet. Eight, you take the next step. The warm water rises past your ankles. You are relaxed. Seven, the warm water has passed your knees, and the sensation travels up to your abdomen and lower back. Six, you take another step into the warm pool. Your chest relaxes. You breathe deeply. Five, the warm water of the pool covers your hands and arms. Four, your neck and shoulders are now immersed in the pool. Three, you are now effortlessly floating in the pool. Two, you breathe deeply and exhale as you float. One, you are completely relaxed. It is November 8. Where are you?"

"At the monastery."

"What are you doing?"

"Teaching."

"What are you teaching?"

"English."

"What do your students call you?"

"Sister Mary Katherine."

"What time of day is it?"

"It's morning, ten o'clock."

"Go forward in time to the evening of November 8.

Where are you?"

Miriam becomes visibly uncomfortable. Doctor Boyd continues.

"You are safe in the water. You are comfortable. Where are you now?"

"Detained."

"Where are you detained, Sister Mary Katherine?"

"Not Sister Mary Katherine, Miriam Davidson."

"Where are you detained, Miriam?"

"I do not know."

"Who detained you?"

"The Gestapo."

"What is the date, Miriam?"

"November 8, 1940."

"Go to the moment that you escaped. How do you escape?"

"Death." Miriam begins to flail.

Doctor Boyd ends the session.

"It appears to me that something so horrific has happened to her that she cannot bear it, so her mind has put this fantasy memory of the Gestapo in place." Doctor Sam offers the analysis that he had readied on the very afternoon that he had decided that Boyd would suit his purpose.

"So, you think that this fantasy that she has created is easier for her to accept than the truth, whatever that may be?" Boyd questioned.

"Yes, Boyd, that's exactly what I think. I think she will eventually remember. But who knows how long it will take?"

"Yes, you are right...I should put that in my report."

"Very good Boyd. I expect your report will be finished tomorrow. I'm meeting with the social worker soon. The girl must be placed somewhere."

"Uh, yes. Of course. Tomorrow."

"Thanks, Boyd. I knew I could count on you." Doctor Sam pats Boyd on his back and returns to his office.

"You look like the cat that swallowed the canary." D looks up from her computer.

"D, how would you like a helper?" Doctor Sam has mischief in his eyes.

"I won't say no to help, but you have something up your sleeve, and I don't know if I like it."

"I want to give the Jane Doe who came in last week a job."

"Jane Doe? Are you kidding?"

"No, I'm not."

"Do you know anything about her?"

"No, I don't." Doctor Sam knew Denise would bluster. He is enjoying this little chat.

"Are you kidding?

"No not kidding."

" Can I at least talk to her first?"

"Of course, you can." Doctor Sam walked to his door then turned back to D. Will you get the social worker on the phone? Give her the message that everything is set for tomorrow. She can come anytime. Thanks, D. You're a dear."

"Don't 'Thanks, D. You're a dear' me yet. If that girl doesn't hop on one foot, she'll be out of here."

Doctor Sam chuckles as he closes his office door and dials Vicky.

"Hello," Vicky answers.

"Hello, Vicky, this is Sam Rubinstein. I'm glad I caught you at home."

"I'm just leaving for the station. What's up, Doc?" Vicky snorts into the phone as she tries to stifle her giggle.

"I was wondering if you might have some time tomorrow to come in and meet our Jane Doe. We call her Miriam, that's all I can tell you so far though."

"I can be there tomorrow around lunch. See you then?

"Of course."

"Goodbye, Doctor."

"See you tomorrow. Thank you, Vicky."

Vicky is anxious to officially meet Jane Doe. Mike, of course, is not anxious about this turn of events. Mike does not share her enthusiasm toward the ladies of the night; he has certainly tried to dissuade Vicky from her decision to take in the young woman. However, Vicky has made up her mind and will not be moved. Miriam will become a part of her life.

Mike has not been very supportive of Vicky's selfless efforts until recently. Joniqua's son had given information to Mike about the murdered teenage boy found on Channel

Side. He also gave information about the Vicente family's involvement with the Mexican drug cartel in Kumquat. The information was enough to put the boy and his mother in the witness protection program. There is a good chance that Vicky might never see Joniqua again, but she has kept her promise.

CHAPTER SIXTEEN

THE BOOKMARK

The bungalow is nestled under a giant mimosa tree and sprawling live oaks in Hyde Park, a quiet historical neighborhood a few blocks from the beautiful Bayshore Boulevard. Vicky parks her car in the driveway.

"Is this your home, Vicky?"

"Yes, Miriam, this is your home, too, now."

"It is very pretty." Miriam can see Sandalphon perched high in the mimosa tree, watching her through the feathery leaves.

"Thanks. It was a mess when I got it, but I worked at it. It's nice and comfy now."

"Comfy?"

"Oh, that's short for comfortable. Don't worry, I'll

teach you. Soon, you'll even have a southern accent." Vicky laughs. She is at ease with her decision to allow Miriam into her home. She trusts old Doctor Sam, besides when she was painting the guest room for Miriam, she realized that she is not only alone, she is lonely.

"A southern accent, ja?"

"Come on in. I think you'll like it."

Miriam winces when Vicky touched her back as she helped her to the door. Most of Miriam's visible wounds are healed, but she is still tender. She also suffers headaches from her head injury, but she never complains.

"This is very close to the hospital. It took only a short time to drive here, this is good. I will walk to the hospital for my job."

"Hold up there sweetie. We're not talking about you walking anywhere just yet. Let's get settled in, and then we can take care of the details, okay?"

"Ja good, Vicky."

"I'm glad you're here. I hope you'll be happy here as well." Vicky gives Miriam a gentle hug.

"My father always said to me, 'Happiness is a choice,'

and you have made an easy choice for me. I will be happy. Thank you. Vicky, do you hear a noise?"

"Oh, I forgot about Rocky."

"Rocky?"

"Come with me."

Miriam follows Vicky through the house to the back door. Vicky opens the door and in bounds a gangly red dog with ears disproportionately large for her head. Vicky taps her chest, and the dog stands on her hind legs and gently rests her front paws on Vicky's shoulders. Vicky kisses the scraggly dog's black nose.

"Miriam, this is Rocky. Rocky, this is Miriam. Miriam lives with us now, so you have to take care of her too, okay?" Rocky's ears rotate like satellite dishes searching for a signal as Vicky speaks.

"I am pleased to make your acquaintance, Rocky." Miriam kneels as the big dog enthusiastically greets her.

"She likes you, and she's not easily impressed." Vicky is also impressed. Rocky isn't just Vicky's dog. She is Vicky's best friend and an impeccable judge of character.

"Then I am honored. I am sure we will be great

friends."

"I put some clothes in your room for you, let's go look." Miriam and Rocky follow Vicky to the guest bedroom. Vicky has chosen a few things from her wardrobe that she thinks Miriam might be able to wear.

"This will be your room, Miriam. Do you like the color?"

"Ja, peach is my favorite color. It is very nice." Miriam nods her approval as she speaks.

"I hope you can wear some of these. I think we're almost the same size. Anyway, these will do for your new job until we can go to the mall."

"Mall?"

"Yes, shopping."

"Oh, shopping. This is good."

Vicky smiles. "Yes, this is good, very good, Miriam."

"Hi, what's up, girl? Boy it was wild at the station today. Must be a full moon." Vicky sits on the edge of Miriam's bed.

"Vicky, I feel this is not right." Miriam turns to Vicky.

"What isn't right? You've only been with me a short time, something can't be wrong already."

"You have been so good to me, and I have kept things from you because we thought you would not understand." Miriam sniffles and wipes her eyes.

"Are you crying? What do you mean 'we'?"

"Doctor Sam, but it's not all his fault. It is all so strange."

Vicky puts an arm around her new friend. "Miriam, sugar, its okay. You can tell me. We'll figure this out, whatever it is." Miriam cries as she takes the rest of the evening to account to Vicky how it happened that she came to be here.

Vicky had taken the old doctor's word that Miriam had no family or friends here. Now Vicky knows that was true enough. She believed the doctor when he said that Miriam was not a danger. Well, the truth of Miriam's story didn't change that either. She is lost as the doctor had said, that's for sure. Doctor Sam had been truthful. Vicky holds Miriam as she sobs.

"So, Doctor Sam figured this out? Who you are and

everything? He said he knew that he knew. Just like my grandmother, I guess he did." Vicky shakes her head. She has a new found respect for the cunning old doctor.

"Ja. He is the only one who knows about me, and now you know."

"I knew you didn't have amnesia. I knew it was bull." Vicky smiled a big self-satisfied grin.

"Bull?"

"Yeah, bull—not real."

"Bulls aren't real now?"

"Sure, bulls are real, Sugar, but… well. It's okay. You're a brave girl. Go to sleep now, don't worry. We'll talk about this more later." Vicky is tired but she will be awake most of the night processing everything that Miriam has told her.

" Is this your first Thanksgiving Sister Theresa Marie?"

"Yes it is Vicky. Thank you for inviting me."

" Please Sister take the seat across from Miriam." Vicky welcomed her guest.

"It's my first Thanksgiving too," Miriam giggled.

In the short time Miriam has been living with Vicky, she has experienced quite a few firsts. Some were odd and quite jarring, like her first ride in hectic interstate traffic and some were pleasant, like watching movies on the flat box that hangs on the wall they called television and now this wonderful big family meal they called Thanksgiving.

"Vicky, you know I am quite fond of your friend." Sister Theresa Marie smiles.

"So am I, Sister. Now, make sure to save room for dessert,"

"Dessert? Are there cookies?" Theresa Marie winks at Miriam.

"Yes, cookies and even pie!" Miriam smiles back at Theresa Maria

Rocky races to the front door, as the door bell chimes.

"That must be Mike. He always comes for dessert on Thanksgiving." Vicky opens the door, and Mike greets Rocky with the expected vigorous pat on her head. The bouquet of flowers and a bottle of wine he holds are, like always, the gifts for the hostess.

"For you, Vicky. Happy Thanksgiving." Mike hands the flowers and wine to Vicky and gives her a quick hug.

"Thank you, Michael."

Mike pulls a chair to the table between Vicky and Miriam. He leans over and gives Miriam a one-armed, big brother-type hug.

"Good to see you, girl. How's the job coming?" Mike is warming to this new living arrangement. He is actually beginning to like Miriam.

"It is good, Mike. I do not work too hard." Miriam smiles.

"É bello vederti di nuovo, Sorella *Theresa Marie*." Mike greets the sister, Italian rolling off his tongue.

"And it is good to see you again, young man," Sister Theresa Marie says.

Mike fixes himself a plate of pumpkin pie, heavy on the whipped cream, and watches Vicky and Miriam as they laugh and talk. He is sure Vicky is keeping something from him. As much as Mike is beginning to like Miriam, he knows something is fishy. His father had always said, "The fish stinks from the head down." Although his father's stinky fish quote was quite colorful, Mike had learned to rely more on his mother's words, "It will all come out in the wash, dear." Mike guesses he will wait for the wash.

After the meal is over, Miriam clears the table and Vicky loads the dishwasher.

"This is a very good thing, this dishwasher. I think I am able to do this by myself. I have watched you often now."

"I think you can give it a try."

"On Sunday, I would like to go to the Holy Trinity. There is going to be a special celebration of mass for the religious treasures display. I know you are on duty but Theresa Marie said that she could arrange for someone to pick me up and bring me home. I feel well, Vicky, and I would really like to go. Do you think that would be all right?" As she speaks, Miriam keeps her eyes on the dishwasher puzzle she is trying to solve.

"Try fitting that platter on the other side," Vicky suggests. That might work. I don't see any reason why you shouldn't go, that will be a nice outing."

"Yes, it will be."

His Eminence Ignatius Duetzman stands in the vestibule of the chapel at the Holy Trinity Monastery. He peers down the long hall. He can see two nuns engaged in conversation. He has known one of the nuns, Sister Theresa Marie, for more than sixty years. The other sister he does not recognize, but she has an air of familiarity. Cardinal Duetzman walks toward the sisters. The young sister glances at the old cardinal, and then she turns and walks away. The cardinal's old eyes, or perhaps the shadows of the dimly lit hall, had played a trick on his mind. *"Of course,"* Ignatius thinks, *"That could not be the young Jew the sisters had called Sister Mary Katherine. No, that would be impossible."*

"Sister Theresa Marie, may I speak to you for a moment?"

"Certainly, your Eminence." Theresa Marie does not bow.

"Is everything ready for the opening of the exhibit? It's only five days from now. Who was that sister you were talking to?" Ignatius strains to watch the young sister.

"Yes, everything is ready, Ignatius. That was a young sister from my convent. She will be helping with the artifacts. I must go now. Excuse me."

Sister Theresa Marie walks the dim halls of the monastery to her room in the private quarters for visiting sisters. Miriam waits there.

"Mary Katherine, I mean, Miriam that was perfect, just as we planned. Ignatius is not sure of what he has seen. Tell me, what's next?"

"I want to see Eliakim. We can talk on the way." As they walk through the monastery's dim halls, Miriam tells Theresa Marie about the night she saw Ignatius murder the man in the courtyard.

"Miriam, I fear there is nothing we can do. That was so long ago."

"You are right, Theresa. It was a long time ago, but I have not told you the complete account of that night. I was certain Ignatius did not know that I had seen what he had done. I quickly crept to the courtyard, keeping to the shadows so I would not be discovered. I followed Ignatius as he dragged the man's body into the grotto and buried him under the trees. When I knew Ignatius had left the monastery for the night, I went to his office. The door was locked, but I knew that his balcony door was always open. I went through the archives room and then out onto the balcony. I climbed over the rail that separated the two balconies. I went to Ignatius's desk in hopes of finding something. I wanted something that I might be able to use against him, a note a journal, anything. I did not know what I was looking for until I came upon a book with a gold marker in it. Engraved on the marker was the inscription: 'To Father Ignatius, Love, Richard.' I put the bookmark in my pocket and hurried back to the grotto. I then dug with my hands into the dirt that covered the man and placed the bookmark there. I planned to expose Ignatius. The bookmark would be the evidence, but the opportunity never arose. But now I have a plan."

"We shall see, Miriam. Now we shall see," the older sister says. "Mass will begin soon. I must take my place." Sister Theresa Marie hugs Miriam and leaves her in the treasures room with Eliakim.

"I will be in soon, Theresa."

Miriam studies Eliakim. His plaster finish is very

much intact, and he has only a few slight scratches. He is none the worse for wear.

Cardinal Duetzman begins the consecration of the cup. His Eminence is miraculously changing the wine to blood. With all parishioners eyes closed, he lifts the cup.

"Take this cup of the New Testament, the blood that was shed for all, for the pardon of all your sins." The cup in Ignatius's hand has not become the elixir that would save their immortal souls. It remains merely a sacristan's concoction of mixed dregs of wine. It would by no means save anyone's soul. Ignatius watches Sister Mary Katherine enter the chapel. She quietly takes a seat next to Sister Theresa Marie.

His Eminence doesn't notice the exact moment that the wine from the cup he holds in his shaking hand splashes onto his white robe. Moreover, for his life, Ignatius cannot see the distinction between the splash of wine and a stain of blood.

"Shake, shake, shake your booty. Shake your booty."
Vicky sings along to the music that blares through her house
as she and Rocky dance. Rocky jumps and hops, following
Vicky as she gyrates around the kitchen.

"Is this a private dance?" Miriam giggles.

"Oh, I didn't hear you come in. How was work? Are
you hungry? I'm thinking about pizza. How's that sound?"

"Ja, pizza would be good. Very good," Miriam calls to
Vicky as she changes from her work clothes. Miriam emerges
in sweats and flip-flops, her first purchase from her first
paycheck, and flops onto the couch.

"What do you want on your pizza? I'm ordering
now."

"Black olives and those salty fishes."

"Anchovies? *Pew!* Only on your half."

"Vicky?" Miriam says. "Do you think you can drive
me to the Holy Trinity?"

"Probably. When do you want to go? Do you want a
salad with your pizza?" Vicky calls back from the kitchen.

"Tonight, and ja, salad please."

"Wait, what? Hold on." Vicky quickly finished the

pizza order. "Tonight? It's getting late. We'll have to hurry!" Vicky stood next to the couch where Miriam had flopped.

"No, not now. I do not care to go so early. I think about one o'clock is good."

"One o'clock in the morning? No, not good! What in the world do you want to do at that hour in the morning at the monastery?"

"There is something there that belongs to me. I will take it back."

"Miriam, you can retrieve your own property that's at the monastery. It's the law. Just ask for it." Vicky looks down at Miriam, wondering what on earth is going through this girl's head.

"Ja this is good. I will go in and ask them for my property. Then they will ask me, 'How is this something yours?' Then I will answer that I made it when I lived in Germany in 1940. Then, they will say, 'Go home, crazy girl!'" Miriam rolls her eyes.

Vicky doesn't argue she could see that Miriam's thinking is based in irrefutable hypothetical logic. "I don't know, Miriam. How long do you think it will take you to sneak in and out again?" Vicky then shakes her head. She can't believe that she is actually considering being a part of breaking into the Holy Trinity Monastery.

"Only a short time. I will be in and out quickly, I promise, I think. Please, Vicky, this is important."

"I can't believe I'm driving you to the monastery in the middle of the night so you can break in. God help me. I think there is a special place in hell for me now." Vicky drives toward Kumquat to the Holy Trinity Monastery.

Miriam sits in the passenger seat with a large Mickey Mouse beach towel folded in her lap, another one of her first purchases. Rocky sits in the backseat with her head out the window, her jowls flapping in the salty breeze. Vicky turns the lights out and parks the car in the alley behind the monastery.

"I'll be here for five minutes and only five minutes, no longer," Vicky cautions. "I'm not fooling, Miriam. I'll leave you after five minutes if you aren't back by then, so you better be in this vehicle buckled up and ready to go in five minutes, hear?"

"Ja, Vicky, five minutes. This is good. I understand." Miriam knows that Vicky wouldn't leave her, but five minutes is all the time she needs. She opens the car door and sprints toward a stand of unkempt bushes.

"Rocky girl, this is not good. What am I doing?" Vicky asks her companion. Rocky's ears rotate. She sticks her nose in Vicky's face for a kiss. Vicky sighs, rubs Rocky's ears, and watches the bushes that Miriam had disappeared into. She looks at her watch. Only two minutes have passed.

"Damn, Rocky, that girl doesn't even have a watch. What was I thinking? Damn, damn, damn." Rocky sticks her cold nose in Vicky's face again. Vicky checks her watch. Three minutes have gone by.

"Rocky, Rocky, Rocky. I can't go to prison. A police officer in prison. Oh Lord." Rocky paws Vicky's shoulder and lays her nose on the back of Vicky's seat.

"Alright, one kiss and then you sit back and settle down, Rocky." Vicky kisses Rocky's nose, and the big red Dingo settles into the back seat. Vicky checks the time again. Four minutes have passed, but it seems like hours. Vicky watches for any sign of Miriam. A huge flash illuminates the night sky, and Rocky jumps into the driver's seat with Vicky.

"Get off me, you big chicken." Vicky pushes Rocky, who stubbornly resists, back into the rear seat. Another flash is followed by a loud, booming sound. Rocky shivers in fear in the backseat.

"You're right, Rocky. That was thunder, not an explosion." Even as she says it, Vicky knows that isn't true. Vicky knows in her heart of hearts that Rocky actually isn't right and it *was* very much an explosion. She hates it when she to has to lie to the dog.

"It was thunder. Oh God, oh God, oh God. That wasn't an explosion. Thunder, it was just thunder. Oh damn, damn, damn, damn." Just as Vicky is in the middle of her breakdown, she sees Miriam running through the bushes, followed closely by a night guard who is wearing only Miriam's Mickey Mouse beach towel tied around his hips.

Of course he is. Why not? Nothing about this night has made any sense anyway. Vicky's mind is boggled. She starts the car and spins around to the place where Miriam would come out of the bushes. The guard is close behind her. Vicky leans over and opens the passenger door.

"Get in, hurry!" Vicky has the motor revved and is ready to speed off. To Vicky's surprise, Miriam opens the rear car door and pushes the half-naked man into the backseat and slams the door.

"Drive quickly." Miriam jumps into the front seat.

Vicky speeds away, fishtailing her way down the narrow alleyway. Vicky speeds down the alley behind the monastery.

"What are you doing? No, who is that? What's going on? Why do I have a half-naked guy in my car?" Vicky speeds down the alleys behind the houses, races across city streets, and turns back to Bayshore Boulevard. She heads toward Hyde Park; she is almost home.

"It is the law, Vicky. He is my property. I have retrieved him." Miriam tries to reassure Vicky.

"Oh God, oh God, oh God."

"Are you praying, Vicky?"

"Hell yes, I am!"

"Oh, I was not sure. I have never heard a Baptist pray before. Was that a stop sign?"

"Stop sign, where? Crap! Maybe no one saw." Red

flashing lights fill the car. "Crap, crap, crap!" Vicky pulls the car over. "Act natural, Miriam." Vicky rolls down her window as the officer walks up.

"Hey, Vicky, I didn't know it was you." The officer, leans into Vicky's window.

"You would have if you had run the plates. You still riding with Zamboni?"

"Yeah, as long as I'm a rookie, I guess that's the program."

"What's the old man doing back there?"

"He's just sittin' I think. Waitin' to retire, you know."

Zamboni nudges the rookie aside and sticks his head in the car window.

"Where you goin' so fast, Vic?"

"We're just out for a ride."

"Hey, I just heard on the radio. There's been an explosion at the Holy Trinity. You came from that way. Did you see anything?"

"No, Zamboni. I didn't see anything. Did you see anything, Miriam?"

"Ja, no, I did not. Did you see anything, Vicky?"

Vicky purses her lips and squints her eyes at Miriam.

Zamboni shines his flashlight around Vicky's backseat, illuminating a curious red dog cautiously sniffing a very well-proportioned, muscular man who is wrapped only in a Mickey Mouse beach towel.

"You're out kind of late, Vic." Zamboni chooses to ignore the bizarre scene in the backseat of his colleague's car.

"Yeah, when Rocky can't sleep, I like to take her out for a little ride," Vicky says. "She loves to stick her head out the window on Bayshore."

"I imagine she does. It smells a lot like garbage," Zamboni retorts as he walks back to his patrol car.

"Vicky needs a break. She's been working too hard lately." The rookie says, the Zamboni nodded in silent agreement.

CHAPTER SEVENTEEN

ELIAKIM

Vicky locks her front door. A half-naked man stands in her living room, and Miriam has some explaining to do.

"Okay, Miriam, *if*—and that's a big if—if I accept your explanation that you created him and then animated him from with some sort of ancient mystic recipe, or something, why would you bring him from the monastery? Wouldn't it have been enough to know that he was there safely on display? Why did you want him?"

"It wasn't him that I wanted, but I had to animate him to get what I did want." Miriam pulls a book from under her sweatshirt. "This is what I wanted."

"What's that?"

"This is the journal my father gave me. In this book

are all of my father's notes about the Kabbalah. I used what he had written in it to create Eliakim."

"Why would you create him?"

"I created him to have a place to hide my father's journal from the Gestapo," Miriam started. "And because I thought there might be a time that I could use the protection of a golem. When I was taken away, Eliakim was left with the journal hidden under his robe. When I found out that he was here, I knew that I had to animate him to retrieve the journal, and then I had to take him with me. All that is left at the monastery are some pieces of clay that were his robe and cloak. His robe and cloak would not animate, of course.

Miriam examines her creation. "Oh, there is a small amount of plaster dust. You see, I put a plaster finish over him for protection. That was my own idea. That was good. See, he looks fine."

"I can't believe I helped you break into the monastery. There's a big hole now in the side of it!" Vicky's voice squeaks, Rocky cocks her head toward Vicky and rotates her ears.

"That I am sorry for, but really, Vicky, we broke out

of the monastery, not in. We could not leave through the door Theresa Marie propped open for me, so Eliakim walked through the side of the building. He is very strong." Miriam announces proudly. She continues studying her golem.

Vicky cradles her head in her hands. She looks at Miriam, then Eliakim, and finally Rocky, who has returned to again sniffing Eliakim. She doesn't know if she is going to laugh or cry or both.

Miriam admires her work. "No one would believe that this is my first golem, ja?"

Vicky snickers. The snicker turns to a giggle, and then the giggle turns to laughter. Tears fall as she laughs.

"You're right about that, Miriam. No one would believe it. Now, what are you going to do with him? Hide him in your closet? Oh okay, actually that's a good idea. He can hand you your sweaters." She laughs all the more.

"That is a good idea, Vicky. Watch," Miriam puts her fingers into Eliakim's mouth and pulls out a small piece of paper. Eliakim immediately turns back to clay.

Vicky stops laughing. Miriam returns the paper to Eliakim's mouth, and he becomes animated once more.

Miriam, Vicky, and Rocky escort Eliakim to his new quarters, deep in the back of Miriam's closet.

It is almost ten o'clock the next morning when the telephone rings. Everyone is asleep.

"Hello," Vicky answers sleepily.

"Vicky, you're not still in bed, are you?"

"What is it, Michael?"

"Just wondering if you heard about the break-in at the monastery last night?"

"Yes, I heard, Michael. That's really something."

"What are you up to today?" Mike hopes that Vicky doesn't have plans so he can drop by later.

"We're cleaning today and then errands." Vicky says. She is really planning to sleep most of the day.

"That's probably what I should do."

"I better get started if I'm going to do what I have planned. See you tomorrow, Michael." Vicky hangs up the phone and puts the pillow over her head.

"Why yes, Michael, we do have a golem hidden in the closet. Thank you for asking," Vicky whispers into her pillow as she falls back asleep.

"Please sit. It's been a while." Doctor Sam offers Paul Linder a chair.

"Was that Jane Doe out there filing papers?" Paul points toward Doctor Sam's outer office.

"Yes, we call her Miriam now."

"She looks good. I know it's been more than a month since I've been here, but I didn't expect her to be, fine, I mean, look so good—I mean, healthy." Paul struggles to find the appropriate words to describe the beautiful young woman he has just seen. He blushes.

"She's doing very well." Doctor Sam smiles. He recognizes the look on Paul's face. He, himself, had been smitten by his beautiful wife Leah so many years ago.

"I would like to talk to her, you know, just about what happened."

"I can tell you now that she doesn't remember anything. Her picture has gone out nationwide and even to Europe. No one seems to know her. Homeland Security has nothing on her. It's as if she fell out of the sky."

"I'm planning to stay in Tampa for a while. A working vacation, sort of. If she has time, I'd still like to get with, ah, talk to her while I'm here."

"That sounds like an excellent idea. I'll speak to Miriam and call you as soon as I have something worked out. Paul, I am curious about something"

'What's that, Doctor?"

"You seem so apt in your profession. I just wonder how long you have been doing this sort of work."

"Well, I took drafting at the university after I graduated high school and then switched to criminal justice. I graduated five years ago and started working with my father. Now, I have taken over the family business. So I guess I've only been doing this officially for five years, but I've been involved since I was a teenager."

"I see. I will get with you as soon as I speak to Miriam. You are a dedicated young man, Paul. Very good, very good."

Paul shakes Doctor Sam's hand. "Thanks, Doctor. Hope to hear from you soon." Paul hopes to hear from the doctor very soon.

Doctor Sam's calculations put Paul's age at twenty-five. He considers Paul Linder. He also considers that Miriam's friend, Sister Theresa Marie, might be interested in Paul Linder and this turn of events too. Doctor Sam begins devising a plan, a good plan, a plan with which he would need Sister Theresa Marie's assistance.

Miriam agrees to meet with Paul Linder in the hospital's atrium. Doctor Sam is surprised at how quickly Miriam had approved of the meeting. Now, Doctor Sam will speak to Sister Theresa Marie about the smitten young man; his plan is coming along nicely. Little does Doctor Sam know that for Miriam's purpose, the meeting with Paul will fit into *her* plan quite nicely. She will conspire with Sister Theresa Marie before the day of her meeting with Paul. Miriam will give her a map to the murdered man's grave and verse her on the particulars of Ignatius crime. Sister Theresa Marie's meeting with the young Nazi hunter will certainly suit Miriam's purpose.

Paul spots Miriam across the atrium. The sunlight streams through the trees, transforming Miriam's hair into a mesmerizing halo.

"Hello, Miriam. My name is Paul Linder." Paul offers his hand.

"Hello." Miriam extends her hand. His incredible good looks are not lost on her.

Paul takes her hand. "I guess the doctor told you why I'm here?"

"Yes, he told me you came earlier, before I was awake." Miriam looks into Paul's soft blue eyes, and her heart skips a beat; crystal white light shone from deep within his soul, a kind heart that she recognizes from a life long ago. *Boog!*

Paul covers her tiny alabaster hand with his free hand and gently turns her palm up.

"Then you know this tattoo on your arm tells me that what happened to you might have been at the hands of the Aryan Nation, the neo-Nazis, or some other group that is hate driven." Paul lightly traces the tattoo as he talks.

"Ja, I know. I am sorry that I cannot tell you anything." Miriam gently pulls her arm back to herself.

Paul sits on the garden bench, next to Miriam,

stretches his long legs in front of himself, clasps his hands together behind his head, and gazes into the brilliant blue Florida sky. He isn't ready to leave Miriam's company yet.

"I've never seen a sky so blue or so high."

Sister Theresa Marie suddenly appears. "Hello, Miriam," she says.

"Sister Theresa Marie! Hello, what are you doing here today?" Miriam feigns surprise. Their plan is on track. Now all Theresa Marie has to do is make an excuse to speak with Paul in private.

"I'm visiting a friend. How are you?"

"I am fine. Thank you. Sister, this is Paul Linder. Paul, this is Sister Theresa Marie."

"I see. It's very nice to meet you, Paul." Theresa Marie smiles at Miriam.

"It's nice to meet you, Sister." Paul stands to greet the sister.

"Will you sit with us for a minute?" Miriam asks.

"Oh, no, I can't. I have much to do. You young people, please continue to enjoy your afternoon. I must return to the monastery. The relics don't take care of themselves.

Actually, you should bring your friend to the monastery to see the display of treasures. I'm certain he would enjoy it." Theresa Marie smiles.

"Thank you, Sister. You're right." A slight smile creases Paul's lips. I think Miriam should give me the guided tour of the monastery. I would love to go to Kumquat and see it."

"Good. Then I will see you soon." Sister Theresa Marie leaves Miriam baffled. This did not go the way that they had planned. Theresa Marie had not followed the plan. How will they ever reveal Ignatius evil deeds unless Theresa follows the plan? Miriam decides go over the details once again with her.

The holiday lights reflect in the dark waters of the Tampa Bay. Green and red lights wrap the palm trees that line the Bayshore Boulevard. Each house that they pass in the quaint little town of Kumquat seems to outshine the one before.

It is Christmas Eve, and Paul has asked Miriam to give him his guided tour of the monastery this evening.

To Paul, the time that passed since he met Miriam in the hospital's atrium has seemed to grind slowly on. Miriam looks beautiful tonight. She is worth the wait. Paul offers his arm to Miriam as they walk from the parking lot to the entrance of the monastery.

The candlelight mass is proudly attended by the Duetzman family. Cardinal Duetzman does not offer mass but rather holds a position of honor at the altar. After mass, Paul and Miriam stroll around the halls of the monastery, admiring the architecture, the antiquities, and the display of relics. They whisper as they walk.

"I'm glad you came this evening. Merry Christmas, Paul, Miriam." Sister Theresa Marie says as she meets Miriam and Paul in the vestibule.

"Merry Christmas, Sister Theresa Marie. Thank you for the invitation. The service was beautiful." Paul bows ever so slightly.

"Please, come to the banquet room. We have set out refreshments." Paul and Miriam follow Sister Theresa Marie into a large room warmed by a fire set in a massive fireplace ornately mantled with carved angles and cherubim.

Sister Theresa Marie understated the holiday feast that was prepared. The tables groan under their burdens. Cookies, cakes, freshly baked pies, and breads are displayed alongside fresh fruit and a variety of nuts, crackers, and pate. Fresh pine branches lay on each table as festive table decorations. A tall evergreen stands in a corner, angels and sparkling white lights decorating its boughs. The crèche sits beneath. As Paul, Miriam, and Theresa Marie enjoy the banquet and each other's company, Ignatius and Richard inch closer to them. Miriam pretends not to notice. Theresa Marie does not notice, and Paul notices only Miriam. Soon, Ignatius and Richard are standing next to the sister.

"Ah, Sister, you have made a beautiful holiday celebration." Even as he is speaking to Sister Theresa Marie, Ignatius keeps his eyes on Miriam.

"Thank you, but I had a lot of help. I could not have done this by myself."

"No, certainly not, and you have invited friends. How nice."

"Yes, your Eminence. This is Paul Linder. Paul, this is His Eminence, Ignatius Duetzman." Theresa purposely excludes Miriam from her introduction.

"Pleased to meet you." Paul extends his hand.

"And I, you. Paul, this is my nephew, Richard Duetzman."

"Good to meet 'cha." Richard runs his hand through his disobedient, aging red hair before he offers it to Paul. Paul's six-foot stature towers over Richard's spindly frame. Richard is a small man by any standard.

"Good to meet you. Merry Christmas, Mr. Duetzman."

Ignatius turns to Theresa Marie. "Sister Theresa Marie, you may remember Richard. He visited the monastery often when he was young."

"Yes, I remember Richard. He was a quite petulant child." Theresa Marie smiles.

"Thanks, Sister. You're a good old gal." Red is inappropriate as usual.

"Richard, will you accompany me across the room? I would like to introduce you to His Grace, the Bishop." Ignatius and Richard make their way back across the room.

"I know I've seen that woman before, but I just can't

place her." Red studies Miriam from across the room. He tries to put a vague remembrance in place.

"She's the spitting image of Sister Mary Katherine. Remember the sister with the raven?"

"Yeah, she is! You should ask her if she's related. She's a dead ringer, that's for sure."

"Don't be a dolt, Richard," the Cardinal snaps. "Do you not understand the danger of that? For all these years, I have thought that Mary Katherine had die. If she somehow survived and this is one of her offspring, then why has she come here? She could cause trouble for me. I'm certain I saw her at mass recently. She looked different then, but I am sure it was her." Ignatius is shaken. He wonders if this woman is simply taunting him, or does she have some information that might be damning? Ignatius cannot afford that possibility.

"Richard, I know you have friends who can make this problem go away. Take care of it."

Richard nods. "I'll speak to Joe."

"Ricardo, to what do I owe the pleasure of this visit?" Joseph Vicente welcomes Duetzman into his Davis Islands home.

"I need a favor, Joe, for my uncle."

"What can I do to help His Eminence?"

"There's a young woman who might have information about him, some damaging stuff. He can't take that chance. She needs to disappear."

"Ricardo, the last time you came to me with woman problems, I had to turn you down. I was sorry. I could have easily had the problem 'taken care' of for you. Unfortunately, because your daughter-in-law's family name is involved with my family name through the sanctity of marriage, I couldn't get involved or I would cause *vendetta famigliare*—family feud." Vicente punctuates his words with his hands.

"I understand."

"I owe you this time, Ricardo. I'll take care of this problem."

"Thanks, Joe. We'll talk later." Richard stands to leave.

"No, no, Ricardo, sit, sit. You must stay. My beautiful Christina is cooking tonight. Stay, *Mangiare*. Eat."

Red sits. It's an offer he can't refuse.

"You'll be able to see the fireworks on Bayshore from the backyard, Miriam."

"Good, I like fireworks."

"I hate to leave you on New Year's Eve, but it's a tradition. Mike and I have always done New Year's Eve together." Vicky primps in the bathroom mirror while Miriam watches.

"You look very nice, sexy."

"Sexy? Where did you hear that?" Vicky laughs.

"On the television," Miriam answers. "That is where I learn about everything like germs and the mouthwash kills ninety-nine percent of the very bad germs and panties that are just my size. It is strange, ja, Vicky? How do you imagine they know my panties size?"

Vicky rolls her eyes but continues her mission in the mirror. Miriam says, "And do you know that most people do not have enough fiber in their diet?" Vicky giggles. "Oh no, Vicky, you must not laugh. This is very serious. It says this on the television often."

"Maybe you watch too much TV, sugar."

"And did you know that people will pay to have food that will make them thin sent to their home? Oh and Vicky, dog food with corn is bad, so don't ever feed it to Rocky. That is important. And a rubber bone will keep her teeth clean. A rubber bone, imagine that? Does Rocky have a rubber bone? Does she have one of those dog jackets that looks like a ladybug?"

"No, she doesn't." Vicky shakes her head at Miriam's chatter.

"Good. I will buy her one. She will look nice in a ladybug jacket, ja?"

"Wow, now I'm sure that you've watched way too much television."

Miriam smiles. "You do look very pretty tonight. Mike will be pleased." She playfully bats her eyes at Vicky, who is taken aback.

"Mike? Why? Mike and I are just friends. Partners, that's all."

"Mike loves you, Vicky. You can see it in his eyes if you look."

"See it in his eyes. Don't be silly, Miriam." Vicky shakes her head yet again, this time at the newest preposterous suggestion.

"Where are you and Mike going?"

"Dinner at the Columbia. What are you going to do?"

"Paul's coming over tonight. He said he must speak to me about Sister Theresa Marie."

"What do you think that's about?" Vicky applies one more coat of mascara.

"They have been talking a lot lately. Maybe she knows something."

"Maybe, or maybe you know something."

"Me? I just got here. I do not know anything yet. Remember?" Miriam crosses her eyes and leans into Vicky's mirror view.

"Right, just don't tell me anything. I haven't recovered yet from ya'll's last scheme." Vicky takes one last look in the mirror before walking out of the bathroom. "Don't wait up for me. I'll be out late." Vicky gives Miriam a playful pat on the cheek as she passes. Miriam follows her to the door.

Vicky opens the door and jumps back. She is surprised to see Paul standing on the porch; she places her hand over her heart for emphasis. Miriam giggles behind her.

"Paul! You startled me. Did you just get here?"

"Yeah, I just got here. Didn't Miriam tell you I was coming?"

"She did. I'm just leaving. Y'all have a nice time. Goodbye. Oh, and Miriam, save your money. No ladybug jackets."

"Ladybug jackets?" Paul repeats.

"For Rocky. Too much TV," Vicky calls out on the way to the driveway.

"Rocky the dog?" Paul attempts to clarify.

"Yes, Rocky is a dog." Miriam explains. "Vicky thinks she's been watching too much TV. I think she drinks too much coffee."

"Vicky drinks too much coffee?"

"No, Rocky." Miriam smiles. "I hope you like to watch fireworks."

"Rocky?" Paul wants to understand, but his critical thinking skills are baffled, so he gravitates towards the familiar. "Yeah, I do. I love fireworks." Paul does love fireworks, but he would have said he loves pearl diving if that was what Miriam had planned.

"Good. Vicky says that we can see them from the backyard."

"Before the fireworks though, I need to talk to you about Sister Theresa Marie."

"What about her?" Miriam asks as she closes the door behind Paul.

Paul waits until they are seated in the living room before speaking again. Miriam's plan is back on track.

"She told me that she witnessed the Cardinal murder a man when he was a young priest. She gave me a map to the location of the man's grave."

"Sister Theresa Marie told you this?" Miriam asks.

"Yes, and she also gave me a suicide note from a young boy who references the Cardinal abusing him. She says that she always suspected that he was secretly a Nazi, but she never had the opportunity to expose him."

"What will you do, Paul?"

"That is why I'm telling you this. Even if you don't

remember there's a chance that you are a nun because when you were found you were dressed in a nun's habit. I like you, Miriam, but I have to turn this information over to the FBI. I can't let my friendship with you stop me from doing what I do."

"It does not matter what I remember or do not remember. Do what you must, and please do not be sorry for seeking justice."

"I just want to say that if sometime you remember that you are a sister, please don't hold this against me. I'm sorry. I would never hurt you, but this man must be exposed."

"I know you would never hurt me, Paul, You must do what you know is right, just like your grandfather did. I am certain that he did not like what he had to do for the Nazis."

Paul hugs Miriam and nuzzles her soft hair, but what she said about his grandfather sticks in his mind. He can't remember talking to her about his grandfather's work. He holds Miriam at arm's length as he searched his memory. Paul is certain he has never spoken of his grandfather or his work.

"How do you know anything about my grandfather? I need an explanation."

"You have his beautiful eyes." Miriam's mind goes to the horrifying night so long ago in Germany. She remembers Boog. She can see in her mind's eye the crystal white light that flashed from his soul and shone out through his eyes that night she allowed him to affix two letters and a string of numbers on her arm.

"We have to talk, girl."

"Ja I will tell you everything…" With Miriam's explanation, that night not only begins a new year for Paul Linder, it also begins a new reality.

The last person Mike expects to see eating alone in the Columbia on New Year's Eve is Victor Duetzman, but there he sits…alone. Mike wants to speak to his old friend, but this is his special night with Vicky. She looks up from her plate.

"What is it, Michael?"

"Victor Duetzman's at the table in the corner. I haven't seen him in years."

"Go say hi to your friend, Michael."

Mike is unsure about this. "He's eating alone on New

Year's Eve."

"All the more reason to go over." Vicky nudges Mike. "I'll be fine by myself for a little. Say hi. Catch up."

"You're right." Mike lays his napkin next to his plate and goes over to his old friend. "Victor. Hey!"

"Mike! I thought that was you." Victor stands, shakes Mike's hand, and then bear hugs him.

"It's been a long time." Mike grins.

"Sit down for a minute."

"How are Cooper and the kids?" Mike takes the seat across from Victor.

"The kids are great. They're growing up. They're six and ten now."

"Six and ten! No, that doesn't seem possible. How's Cooper?"

"She's good, but Coop and I aren't together anymore."

"I'm sorry to hear that. What happened?"

"She couldn't take it. It's my own fault. I wasn't strong for her. I would still have my family if I had been the man I should have been."

"She seemed like a nice girl."

"She is nice, too nice. My family made her life a living hell. My brothers and sisters were ruthless. My father especially hated her. It was disgraceful. You know, my family has everything money can buy. They want for nothing, but they hated my wife because she has something that they do not have, something they could not buy and they couldn't take from her. Do you know what that one thing is, Mike?"

"What, Victor?"

"Virtue, Mike. It's virtue."

CHAPTER EIGHTEEN

GASPARILLA

"I'll never get used to Eliakim. He scares the beejesus out of me when I come home and he's awake." Vicky tosses her car keys onto the entry table.

"He only does what I tell him to do, so, ja, I guess you better be careful then." Miriam laughs.

"Not funny. What if he got mad and went crazy or something?"

"That cannot happen. There is nothing in his head. You know, poor thing, if I only had a brain." Miriam makes circling motions around her temples with her fingers as she sings the scarecrow's refrain. Miriam had recently taken the opportunity to watch *The Wizard of Oz* each and every time it had been shown on the movie channel.

"Way, way too much television, Dorothy!" Vicky calls from her room.

Miriam continues humming as she puts the finishing touches on Eliakim's fresh attire. Now, instead of the Mickey Mouse beach towel tied around his waist, Eliakim sports black spandex biking shorts, a gray tank top, and a Tampa Bay Rays baseball cap.

"There, done. Come see how nice he looks, Vicky."

"That's better than the towel." Vicky returned to her room.

"Is something wrong? Did I tease you too hard? I promise Eliakim will never hurt you."

"No, it's just, I've been thinking about what you said about Michael, that he loves me, seeing it in his eyes, and all. I think you're right, and I don't know what to do about it."

"Vicky, maybe there is nothing for you to do. Just let love take care of itself."

Vicky gave Miriam a tight hug. "Miriam why are you so smart?"

"Because I only have a brain," Miriam squeaks.

"Well, Sugar I've got Gasparilla duty I'll see you this

evening."

"See you later. I'm going to watch it on the television."

"I imagine you are."

Gasparilla—the celebration of the taking of Tampa by the bloodthirsty pirate José Gaspar.

José Gaspar, as legend tells raped, sodomized, and murdered men, women, and children and then pillaged and burned the city until it fell into submission. Of course, the celebrants will tell you, "It's only a legend. Pure myth. No truth to it whatsoever." This leaves them celebrating the idea and spirit of plunder, rape, sodomy, and murder.

The Tampa elite, in all probability, are generally good and civilized people, merely with a dedicated sense of style and an over exaggerated penchant to be well put together. Oddly however, in drunken revelry, the Tampa influential have dressed themselves in garish costumes to celebrate Gasparilla for more than a century

The Gasparilla celebration has begun. The pirates have invaded Tampa. The keys to the city have been surrendered to the pirate captain. The mayor and the police chief are in the dungeon, and chaos rules. Pirates and scantily-clad wenches parade down Bayshore Boulevard. Rowdy pirate men, pirate women, pirate children, and pirate dogs and cats mill through the crowds.

Mike and Vicky work crowd control. Mike works the east side of Bayshore Boulevard, and Vicky works a few blocks farther north on the west side of the street.

"Vicky, Vicky!" Joniqua runs toward Vicky, waving her arms desperately, trying to get her attention. She fights her way through the throng of revelers and stands in front of Vicky and blurts out her horrific message. "Vicky! I had to come. I had to warn you. Vicente put a hit on your friend Miriam."

Vicky's eyes widen. "Are you sure?"

"Vicky, yes I'm sure. One of Vicente's girls told me to warn you. There's no time. The guy's been sent today. I just found out. You have to hurry. There's no time."

Vicky pulls her cell phone from her pocket and dials her home.

"Pick up, Miriam. Pick up, pick up," she murmurs to

herself.

"Hello?"

"Oh, thank goodness, Miriam. Are you okay? Are the
doors locked?"

"Yes. Are you still at that Gasparilla thing?"

"Hush, Miriam. Listen to me."

"What's wrong?"

"Is Eliakim awake?"

"Yes, he is. You are frightening me. What is wrong?"

"Someone has been sent to our house to kill you!
Get out of the house! Get out quick! Run toward Bayshore.
I will find you, I promise. Just run fast, Miriam!" The phone
falls from Miriam's hand. Vicky can hear the sound of
glass breaking and Rocky barking wildly before the phone
disconnects.

"Eliakim! Protect me," Miriam shouts. She points to
the man dressed as a pirate who had broken the glass and was
trying to push open the kitchen door. Without a backward
glance, she runs out the front door and heads toward
Bayshore.

The hit man pushes open the door just as Eliakim

reached the kitchen. He fires two shots directly into Eliakim's head, but Eliakim keeps walking toward him.

"What the hell?" the man says. He fires one more shot and then turns and runs back through the kitchen door.

Eliakim follows while Sandalphon circles above. Certain that he did not miss his target, the hit man was unsure of exactly what had just happened, but he is determined to catch up with his intended mark. The hit man, dressed as a pirate, appears to be one of the celebrants as he runs through the crowd. When he catches the girl, he will finish his job, and the happy crowd of revelers, thinking that he and the girl had been part of the festivities, and will be none the wiser.

Vicky radios to Mike. "Code 2! Code 2! Mike, watch for Miriam. She will emerge on to Bayshore from West Bay Street or thereabout. Advise on her location and the direction she is heading. Copy?"

"Copy. I see her and Rocky now. She's running through the crowd on the west side of Bayshore, heading toward the Platt Street Bridge. They're a block north of you."

Vicky runs toward Miriam, and Mike runs to back up

his partner. Miriam and Rocky continue running toward the Platt Street Bridge.

The hit man is catching up to Miriam when Rocky turns and jumps, hurling herself into the path of the hired killer. With one powerful movement, the assassin catches Rocky in midair, flings her to the pavement, and continues running. Vicky is heart broken as she runs past Rocky lying motionless on the pavement; she pushes herself forward to catch up. Vicky can see Miriam. She can also see the assailant getting closer, but he has been slowed down a bit thanks to Rocky's bravery. Now, Vicky can catch up to him before he catches Miriam.

Exhausted, Miriam reaches the bridge, the hit man following close behind. She tries to continue running along the sea wall, but her aching body fails her. Miriam stumbles and falls, the gunman takes aim.

"Police, drop your weapon! Turn around, and drop your weapon!" Vicky holds her gun on the hit man. He drops to the ground, firing shots. Eliakim walks through a firestorm of bullets. The hit man turns his gun toward Miriam, but a crushing grip prevents him from firing. Eliakim lifts him from the pavement by the throat and effortlessly holds him over his head. One sharp snap and the assassin grows limp. Eliakim effortlessly tosses the dead pirate over the sea wall.

The crowd engulfs Eliakim and Miriam as they cheer the Gasparilla hijinks. As the celebrants shout with delight and the pirate floats into the bay Mike cradles Vicky's body as he makes a frantic cry into his radio.

"Officer down! Officer down! I need an ambulance! My partner is down! I need assistance! Please! Platt Street Bridge! Officer down!"

Miriam sits beside Paul. Mike and David Knowles sit silently at her other side. Paul tenderly holds her hand to comfort her. The words that Miriam hears—"suddenly taken," "loved by many," "will be greatly missed"—make no sense to her. They bring no comfort; she grieves the loss of her friend. After the service, when all the condolences have been given, Mike excuses himself. Only Paul and Miriam remain seated.

"Will you go to the monastery today?" Paul speaks in hushed tones.

"Ja, I will," Miriam says. They will meet again very soon.

Miriam opens the front door. Vicky's house is quiet. Eliakim stands in a dark corner. Miriam crosses the room. She takes a small piece of paper from Eliakim's pocket, and puts it in his mouth.

"We are going to the monastery, Eliakim, as soon as I change."

Miriam walks the quiet hall to her room and opens her closet. With each item of clothing that she puts on, she once again becomes Sister Mary Katherine.

Miriam kneels at the altar with her back to the confessional and waits for the parishioner to leave. A few moments pass, and the confessional door opens. The parishioner thanks His Eminence and hurries away. The parishioner glances back as he reaches the chapel doors. Ignatius walks to the altar.

When Miriam feels Ignatius standing behind her, she

stands and turns to face him. His eyes widen as he steps back.

"What do want from me? Who are you?"

"I think you know who I am." Miriam steps toward Ignatius.

"No, I have never seen you before."

"You have, but perhaps you have you forgotten."

"No, no," he whispers, "Why do you haunt me?" Ignatius stumbles but does not fall.

"Only a ghost can haunt. Do you think I am a ghost? Look at me. I am flesh and blood. I am alive." With each step Miriam takes toward Ignatius, he takes one back toward Eliakim, who stands in the shadows.

"Will you hear my confession again, Your Eminence?" Miriam takes another step.

"Again? No, I have never heard your confession before. You have mistaken me for someone else, young woman." Ignatius steps back.

"I make no mistake, Ignatius. You must have forgotten," Miriam says. "It was so long ago when last you heard my confession, so let me remind you. The Holy Scripture teaches that anyone who does harm to one of God's own would have a better fate if a millstone were hung around their neck and they were cast into the sea. Mother Gertrude and Stephen will be your millstone. I bid you good night, Father." Miriam turns away.

"Tell me where the note is!" Ignatius screams. The old cardinal lunges toward Miriam. His flailing arms grapple Miriam's waist, and the two fall to the floor.

Eliakim steps from the shadows, grasps Ignatius by the back of his neck, and lifts him from the floor. Eliakim dangles a squirming Ignatius by the throat. Ignatius digs at Eliakim's hand, struggling to loosen its hold. Slowly, Miriam picks herself up from the monastery floor and stands beneath the writhing old Nazi.

"Do not kill him yet, Eliakim. I must introduce you first, Eliakim, this is His Eminence Cardinal Duetzman. Cardinal Duetzman, this is my golem, Eliakim. He is the creature that you and your Nazi comrades sought, the prize you desired. He is the statue that stood in the monastery for decades, holding beneath his robe Stephen's note. Do you think you can take the note from him, Ignatius?"

Ignatius struggles to speak but makes only desperate

rasping sounds.

"I created him, and I control him. I can have him crush you." Miriam hesitates. Ignatius squirms.

"Eliakim, now,"

Ignatius' plea is nothing more than a whimper.

"Release him."

Eliakim releases his grip, and Ignatius falls to the floor. Miriam and Eliakim walk down the long hall, through the monastery doors, and down the steps to the waiting taxi.

"Are you going back to the same place, Sister?" the driver asks.

"Yes, but wait for a few minutes please."

Miriam waits in the parked taxi. A few minutes later, a car pulls into the monastery parking lot. Four men in dark suits meet a fifth man at the monastery door. The five men enter the monastery. A short time later, Miriam watches Paul Linder and four FBI agents escort His Eminence in handcuffs from the monastery to the waiting car.

"How's Rocky?" Vicky's breath is labored. Mike has been at the hospital every day since Vicky was shot. The hit man's bullet went in at an angle under her vest. It did a lot of damage, but she will recover.

"I told you she'll be fine. Don't worry." Mike gently brushes Vicky's matted hair to the side.

Vicky closes her eyes. "You're not just telling me that so I don't worry, are you?"

"I'm not just telling you that. She has a few broken ribs, but she's recovering at the animal hospital. She'll be jumping around in no time."

"How was the memorial service for Doctor Sam?"

"It was nice. There were so many people that some had to stand in the hall."

"A massive heart attack." Vicky shakes her head. "It was so sudden. He was a good man. I'll miss him. How's Miriam taking it?"

"Hard. So is Doctor Knowles, and the secretary is a mess."

"What about the detective exam, Mike?"

"Well, Vicky, I don't know. With everything and you in the hospital, there hasn't been a lot of time."

"Michael! I can't believe you! You wanted that so

badly."

"Wanted what? This?" Grinning Mike flashes his shiny new detective badge.

"Michael, you did it! I'm so proud of you."

"We won't be partners now though. You'll probably get the rookie." Mike laughs.

"Not partners...Now what?"

"Now I tell you that I love you. I will always love you, Vicky."

"I know."

Mike raises his eyebrow. "How do you know?"

Michael tenderly kisses Vicky.

"I looked into your eyes."

PROLOGUE

Grace Love Standard—that's what my mama named me, but my daddy always called me Gracie. I'm not sure now if I still have a name since there's no one around to call me to dinner or get me up in the morning. "Gracie it's time to eat." "Gracie wake up, rise and shine." No, I can't say that I hear much of that lately.

I have two things to say right off the get go. I'm dead and I'm not a whore, that's pretty much all I have on my mind these days, but I don't really remember much about that last day. You're probably thinkin', what are you doin' still here, bein' dead and all? Oh I know all about that go into the light, move on stuff but I'm kind of havin' a good time here in Kumquat, now. They can only kill you once I've heard, and yep it's true.

Kumquat is a sleepy little town of five thousand residents, soon to be five thousand and two. Jerri Thompson is pregnant again—twins this time. I think that three thousand five hundred, of the five thousand residents are in the witness protection program. The fifteen hundred remaining folks don't have a clue. The town takes its name from the kumquat that grows in abundance there. The kumquat is a small citrus fruit with a sugary sweet outside and an inside that is bitterly unpalatable, much like the townspeople. Well, that's just my opinion, but as in life, so in death. An opinion doesn't count for much, it's just an opinion.

My very first day in Kumquat, Florida is when I realized what a small town I had moved to. What happened is...

My dog Spider chased a flock of chickens into town. Really, I'm not kidding, but I do admit that was my fault, because you can't fault a dog for being a dog. Anyway, it wasn't only the fact that the town's people knew it was my dog that chased the chickens into the general store; but they also knew that the flock of chickens belonged to that old Miss Wallace. Well, that was my first insight, but the final realization came two weeks later.

I'll tell you right up front I'm not opposed to guns. Nor do I have anything against snakes, but they are right up on top of my squish list. That cottonmouth that slithered out from underneath my house should have waited for me to go back inside. Well, Mama always said dynamite comes in small packages. I figure she was referring to me. So maybe that snake thought that my five-foot-two and a half inches didn't pose a real threat. Better think again, bubba. Of course I don't really know what snakes think, at least I didn't then. Anyway two shots from Lyle, my 38, and the snake was headless. It was what happened right after the snake showdown that really set me straight about Kumquat.

My telephone that was installed only the day before rang. As I live and breathe or don't live and breathe, guess I gotta' get used to that, this is how the conversation went.

"Hello."

"Hello, little lady," The deep voice of a Southern gentleman greeted me "This is the sheriff. What you shootin' at, darlin'?"

"Crap!" I thought. I don't even know my phone number yet, but the sheriff does. This isn't good. Not that I have anything to hide from the law, but one would just generally think that this isn't good.

"A snake." I answered.

"Did ya get 'em?"

"Yes, sir, I did." I was pretty proud of my shootin'. Daddy taught me to shoot one Sunday morning before church, whilst we were sitting on the back porch waitin' for Mama.

The sheriff chuckled. "There were two shots."

He must bored, I thought.

"The first shot was a warning shot." I answered. I heard the sheriff chuckle again.

"Whatcha' usin'?" He asked. Yeah he's bored I decided.

"Lyle, my 38." I was startin' to kinda' like the sheriff.

"You call your gun Lyle?"

"Sure do, 'cause he sings so pretty." I was wishin' that Lyle was my cowboy man.

"I call mine Horace 'cause I bought him from Horace."

"Horace? I haven't had the pleasure." I cooed.

"You use rat shot?" The sheriff asked.

"No, just bullets." I knew he'd be impressed.

"Well, little lady, if you'd used rat shot you'd got 'em on the first shot."

"Where do I get me some rat shot around here?"

"Horace's Guns and Ammo."

"Thanks for the tip sheriff."

"Sure enough, little lady. See you at Horace's."

I really did like the sheriff.

I'm still at the house where I lived, when I lived. The house is an ramshackle old roadhouse; that's polite talk for whore house. I'm really not surprise that I'm still here at the old house, even with being dead and all. You know I had a suspicion from the beginning that the house was spooked, but I didn't care much. My whole family carries on with ghosts, especially Mama did. Mama went on ahead many years ago. I'm pretty sure that when Mama saw the light she didn't walk into it she ran and never looked back. I always thought that she would be there to lead me over when my time came, but I haven't seen her around any. I did see an old cowboy one day, but that was while I was still amongst the living.

It was late in the afternoon. I hadn't slept well the night before. The sound of laughter, music, and dancing kept me awake pretty near most the night. The sounds were bothersome, but I had made a deal with the spirits that shared their home with me. It was settled. They would leave me alone. I would look after the place and they would have a hi-oh time at night while I slept. Not the best deal I've ever struck.

It was the dancin' that I was mainly thinkin' about that afternoon. I was wonderin' if Lyle Lovett liked to dance. I was hopein' he didn't. You see I've never been much of a dancer. I have some trust issues, so the thought of being led around backward with my eyes closed doesn't really appeal to me.

So, I was thinkin' that there should be some kind of a dance intervention clinic. Just in case Lyle does like to dance. I had the notion that the clinic could be run by a dance intervention professional. The clinic's therapy would consist of fallin' backwards blindfolded into a trusted partner's arms. I figured I would begin my dance therapy by fallin' to a nice waltz, then move on to fallin' to a samba, and finally graduate to fallin' to a spirited rumba. Well, I was just thinkin'.

"Anyway, just when I was getting' ready to fall back into Lyle's arms, I heard a ruckus comin' from the chicken coop. I ran out the back door. I was determined to get that fox that was studyin' for my chickens. I ran passed the old abandoned bath house to the chicken coop that sits at the edge of my property. Surprisingly I found the chickens just doing regular chicken stuff. Bittie, Dot, and Penelope were waging their never ending nest wars. Powder, and Bertha were chasing down a big tasty roach, and Clementine and Penny were fighting over bits of lint. It was *always* something with those two. The whole lot was normal. I started back to my house.

As I passed the old bath house I heard a noise coming from inside. I thought it was probably a possum makin' a home in the junk that I had stashed in there, so I picked up a big stick and opened the door. Taken aback I stood in the open door and stared at a weathered cowboy, wearing a ten gallon hat, bathing in an old copper tub.

"Close the door you're lettin' in a draft." He called out in a gravelly voice. I ran back to my house, like there was no tomorrow. A few days later my curiosity got the best of me. I went back to the bathhouse and opened the door a crack and peeped in. The cowboy was there, just like before.

"Are you in or out, Missy?"

"I-i-in I guess." I sputtered.

I sat on a stool in the corner of the dusty bath house and regained my composure.

"Wha wha what are you doin' here?" So much for composure.

"Bathing. Are you blind, girl?"

"No, what–are–you–doin'- here?" I didn't want to be rude and just blurt out "You're a ghost," in case he didn't know. So I thought I should ask him again very slowly.

"Bathing–are–you-blind–girl?"

"Why are you here?" I thought I'd better just start over."

The cowboy leaned forward and pushed his hat back."

"I'm dancin' with Miss Fancy tonight and I paid an extra nickel for this bath. Miss Fancy is expecting me, so if you'll excuse me now, Missy…" With that the cowboy disappeared.

I walked back to my old roadhouse. That night I slept well, knowin' that the sound of laughter and distant music is just the weathered old cowboy leadin' Miss Fancy around backwards with her eyes closed.

Please, continue to enjoy my stories.

JE

www.ingramcontent.com/pod-product-compliance
Lightning Source LLC
Chambersburg PA
CBHW020324140726
47905CB00012B/305